THE MARQUIS OF MOOIKLOOF
and other stories

The Marquis of Mooikloof

and other stories

Sean O'Toole

DOUBLE
STOREY
a juta company

*To mom and dad,
with thanks*

*Grateful acknowledgements to Joan Hambidge, Nele Hopfmann,
Jo Ractliffe, Henk Rossouw and Ivan Vladislavic*

First published 2006 by Double Storey Books,
a division of Juta & Co. Ltd,
Mercury Crescent, Wetton, Cape Town

© 2006 Sean O'Toole

ISBN-10: 1 77013 097 7
ISBN-13: 978 1 77013 097 5

All rights reserved. No part of this book may be reproduced
or utilised in any form and by any means, electronic or
mechanical, including photocopying, without permission
in writing from the publisher.

Edited by Alfred LeMaitre
Page layout by Claudine Willatt-Bate
Cover design by Russell Stark
Printed by Paarl Print, Paarl

Contents

The marquis of Mooikloof	1
An African grey	11
Waiting for Mister President	22
A gift of stones I	41
A gift of stones II	55
A gift of stones III	64
The magic of numbers	74
A chance meeting	85
The road to Rephile	98
Incident report	111
The trophy mount	124

The marquis of Mooikloof

My neighbour introduced himself by way of a newspaper headline. DEPOSED DESPOT SETTLES IN PRETORIA read the news bill attached to a stop sign on my morning route to work. In all honesty, the printed words did not immediately stir much interest, even if the name Saddam Hussein did somewhere flicker in the darkness of my mind. Also, I am not in the habit of buying the morning edition of the *Pretoria News*. So it was only later that morning, during the weekly production meeting I chair, that the headline became an actuality, its contents fleshed out, my new neighbour probed and dissected with instruments of perfect bluntness: words.

Not that I listened to what they were saying at first; their talk was simply adornment, wallpaper of an indistinct pattern. My attentions were focused on the paperwork stacked at the head of the boardroom table where I sat. The imprecise mass of white paper described the extent of my life for the rest of the week. I took a sneak preview. There were eight complaints about our new steam-press iron from retailers. Looking through the complaints, my thoughts were focused on discerning the unseen thread that would bind together all the disparate narratives of discontent, all of them handwritten on our standardised complaints form.

'Did you see the size of his house?' Alet Bothma remarked, with a gruff Benson & Hedges growl, to Mpho Nthebe.

'Ja,' Daan interjected, not allowing Mpho to respond.

Alet glowered at him. Since the last Christmas function, she always scowled at him. Daan pretended to review his notes. Sensing that she could enter the conversation, Mpho shyly asked a question.

'Where is it?'

'Wait, I'll get the paper,' Alet replied, slipping from the wood-panelled boardroom, returning almost instantaneously clutching a copy of the morning edition.

'Look, here it is,' she said pointing with a crimson talon.

After a considered pause, Daan asked for the paper. In a stumbling voice he read excerpts of the story out loud.

'The sumptuous new residence is situated in the plush gated community of Mooikloof ... blah, blah, blah ... According to Marge de Villiers, an estate agent with RE/MAX Properties, the house has an estimated value of R12 million.'

Daan whistled incredulously.

'Mooikloof, Mike, isn't that where you live?' he asked cautiously.

'Pardon?'

'They say here that Robert Mugabe bought a place in Mooikloof. Isn't that where you live?'

'What? Sorry, Daan, I wasn't following.'

Dragging himself from his seat, Daan waddled across the room, dropping the newspaper article in front of me. He pointed to a bright, sunny photograph of a house. It was the house next door; I immediately recognised the ostentatious Corinthian columns.

'Who did you say had moved in?' I asked.

'Robert Mugabe.'

Suddenly it all made sense: the nervous sound of helicopter rotor blades cutting through the mid-morning air, the strange flotilla of vehicles (three moving vans, a dark Mercedes and some police vehicles too) coming up my drive. At the time, the convoluted ritual hadn't struck me as odd. Maybe a government minister, moving in next door. Pretoria hadn't changed much over the years, the only difference between now and back then the way power was displayed – with Corinthian columns.

But this wasn't some petty public works minister promoted from a rural fiefdom. I had read the Sunday papers, I knew who this man was. He was the one callers to radio phone-ins simply referred to as Mugabe, much in the way they referred to Nelson Mandela as Madiba. But this man was different. He was the murderer of Matabeleland, the butcher of Bulawayo. He was the pregnant promise they emblazoned across a thousand T-shirts. The deafeningly wet roar of Victoria Falls. An evolving idea that wouldn't name itself. The immaculately dressed lunacy of Chairman Mao. And now here he was playing a new role, the marquis of Mooikloof.

The production meeting, if you'll excuse the wisecrack given my company's line of business, was a heated one. Immediately afterwards, I had Mpho call my estate agent. She assured me that her comparison of Mooikloof to London's Hampstead was entirely plausible.

'Exiled aristocracy tend to add prestige to an area,' she argued with unconvincing gusto.

That evening, as I passed through the security boom, I decided to take a diversion. I wanted to see Mooikloof anew, marvel again at its discreetly private intimacy. I slowly manoeuvred my Volvo through the near deserted suburban streets, past a series of flawless tributes to deceased architectural styles (English Tudor, Zuid-Afrikaansche Republiek, Cape Dutch, Tuscan and others less easily defined). A voice on the radio tabulated stock figures. I passed a house with two elephant skulls flanking the entrance gate. The woman on the radio tried to convince me to change my cellular phone brand. Two women on horseback waved as they approached from the opposite direction. The talk show host returned, and purposefully set about cajoling a reluctant member of parliament. I drove in silence, drowning in this multitudinous splendour of voices.

As I finally pulled up to my drive, I paused on the kerbside. I looked at the residence next door. It was then that I saw the private security guard sulkily doing nothing at the gates. Dressed in a jet-black uniform, the darkly tanned man – he was white with a thick moustache – carried a shotgun slung over his shoulder. I waved, hesitantly. He simply declined his head in vague acknowledgement of my gesture. I buzzed open my gate.

My house is a vacant emotion, a mouth with no teeth. I am divorced. Two years ago. I suppose it just happened, the way Coke goes flat in the fridge. You wish it didn't, but it just happens – and then you have to throw it away. Susan now lives in

London. We occasionally email one another; her correspondence is always rushed. She has remarried. Susan once sent me a Jpeg image of her husband. He had bleached features, an unfamiliar whiteness. She recently mentioned that she was pregnant. I haven't yet responded to this bit of news, sent an email complimenting her on the small, swelling ambition in her belly. The complaints against our new iron are growing.

I switched on the television, listlessly flicked through the satellite channels. I eventually settled on the repeat broadcast of a recent golf tournament. There is something comforting about knowing the outcome of things. I watched Tiger's approach shot, knowing full well that it was the necessary prelude to a glorious birdie. Despite the pleasure of watching his elegant swing, I found that I was unable to concentrate on the action. I was thinking about him, the man next door.

Why South Africa? And, for that matter, why Pretoria? Why Mooikloof Estate? What about that palatial villa overlooking the solitude of the Atlantic seaboard, in Cape Town? The newspapers had been full of it. Far from resolving things, each question simply elicited another. How did *he* find out about Mooikloof? Surely *he* hadn't been alerted to the development by a neatly dressed tout handing out flyers at a busy intersection on a Saturday morning? I stared at the eutrophic sadness of the watery golf trap on the screen. I switched off the television.

The view from my balcony overlooks a grassy nothingness, veld surrounded by walls, walls encompassed by more walls, like stratified rock. I leant dangerously over the railing, craning my neck. I felt myself unavoidably drawn to the Mugabe residence. The lights of the house were on. He was in.

I tried to imagine a gaunt and ageing figure seated at the dinner table, quietly conversing with his wife, Grace. He was describing his longing for all that had been lost, not simply in terms of assets but emotions, sunsets at Lake Manyame. Grace had a tear in her eye. Or maybe he was simply watching DSTV, glad to be rid of the unending gaze of the camera. Maybe he too was marvelling at Tiger's stoic brilliance, had cheered as the young golfer effortlessly collected his birdie. Then again, he would probably disapprove of golf, the wasted opportunity vast tracts of fertile land presented to his inordinately stern socialist conscience.

More than likely he was watching the news, flicking between CNN, BBC, Sky and SABC Africa, searching for something approximating the truth of his recent demise, something other than the waning graph of his political fortunes. Or maybe he wasn't as timorous as all this; maybe he was engaged in a one-way shouting match, with Larry King, or the BBC's Tim Sebastian, spittle and exasperation running down the flatness of his television screen. Maybe.

Then again it was possible that Grace had commandeered the controls: they were both watching Fashion TV.

I pulled up a chair, the dusky evening silence a warm and incomplete embrace. I wondered what the house looked like inside. Could three vans really contain the totality of a life? Where was the booty? I vaguely recalled seeing the news on television, his 48-hour ultimatum, leave or face prosecution. I wondered how many of her Ferragamo shoes Grace had left behind; Susan had once jokingly mentioned that Grace wore

Ferragamo before asking me to get her a pair on my business trip to Italy. Back then.

And that jet, bought from Hugh Hefner. Where was it parked? At Waterkloof airbase? And rather more importantly, had they met with the silk-robed porn king, laughed and shared a joke as Bunny girls refilled fluted glasses. Facts. Imagination. Multiplicity. I was intrigued. I resolved to invite the couple for a braai.

I shared my thoughts with Mpho and Alet the next morning. It was a rare accident of history, I explained, a privilege even, I added, that I could have Herr Hitler and Eva Braun over to dinner. Mpho simply took notes as I spoke. Alet, however, intermittently coughed up bits of phlegm and incomprehension. I asked Mpho to get quotes for the production of a handmade invitation. My instructions to her were meticulous and detailed: ornate lettering handwritten on a thick grade of white linen paper with the company logo discreetly embossed on it. Our logo is an antique iron.

Pushing aside the complaints, which had increased by three, I spent the entire morning crafting an invitation message, something appropriate to the stature of my potential guest, and his wife. It wasn't easy. There was the problem of my surname – Smith – but that could not be undone. At least I wasn't an Ian. Another problem related to the correct title of my guest. Was I to refer to them as His and Her Excellency, or simply Mr and Mrs? After much wrangling and inconclusive web trawling, I resolved to simply go with the latter. It seemed more neighbourly, to be casual, less of a spectator.

And then it was finally done.

Dear Mr and Mrs Robert Mugabe,

Mike Smith would like to welcome you to Mooikloof and requests the pleasure of your company for an informal Sunday luncheon at his private residence. In the interim, should you require any assistance and advice related to your move to Mooikloof, please feel free to call him at any time.

Yours sincerely,
Michael R. Smith

PS: Please do not hesitate to alert your host should you have special needs or dietary requirements.

The invitation also specified a date, set one month in advance, as well as my address (with the words 'Next Door' in parentheses). Finally, I further included my home and work telephone numbers, also an email address and my company's website, www.newafricaelectronics.com. I was undecided on this last point, worried that it would come across as crude. Daan, however, suggested that it subtly alerted the reader to my credentials; Mugabe, or his secretary presumably, could peruse my biography from the website.

The invitation took three days to complete. I ordered three copies, two just in case I slipped up when I signed the invitation in my own hand. Finally satisfied that the invitation fulfilled all that I would expect were I to receive a similar request, I resolved to drop it off at the Mugabe residence.

'Can I help you, sir?' the guard asked in a flat Afrikaans accent as I got from my car. I had pulled up on a thin sliver of grass between the road and the elevated walls obscuring the Mugabe home.

Looking over his shoulder at the mute white walls he guarded, I explained that I was dropping off an invitation.

'There is no visitors allowed, sir, unless by appointment.'

I told him I had none.

'You will have to leave the delivery with me, then.'

Disappointed, I nonetheless left the invitation at the front gate. Unsure of the guard's qualities, I requested proof of my delivery. The guard disappeared into the hut, returning with an estate agent's card bearing his name on the rear. Gerrie Viljoen, the untidy scribble read. I thanked him, shook his hand. I had bridged the divide.

A week passed during which I could think of nothing but the impending braai. Even though I had not yet heard any word, I nonetheless threw caution to the wind and called my favourite butcher. I ordered handsomely: A-grade beef from the Waterberg region, specially filleted Karoo ostrich sosaties, a piquant Vrystaat boerewors as well as two free-range chickens marinated in peri-peri. I would complement the meat with a basic serving of mielie pap, maybe a selection of veggies. Even though I hated it, milk tart would serve as the exit cue to my intentionally unpretentious Pretoria welcome. If the meal went well, I would invite them to something more sumptuous (and, by all accounts, familiar) at the Westcliff.

I waited on a response, just as I did when Susan left me. I measured out my life with coffee spoons, lingered in front of the television.

Returning one day from work, I saw Gerrie frantically waving as he ran towards me. I eased my car window open.

'Hello, sir,' he panted. His moustache was gone.

'Mr Mugabe's secretary asked me to give you this.'

Gerrie handed me an envelope with my name neatly typed on the outside.

'Thank you,' I said, unsure whether to offer him a cash tip. Eventually we simply smiled at each other.

It was already dark as I pulled into the garage. I turned off the ignition, allowed myself to soak up the darkness, the silence, the weight of the envelope on my lap. I picked up the envelope, gently, weighing it again in the palm of my hand. Susan left nothing when she slipped through the gates, past the walls, into the world outside, not even a note, just belated emails, untouchable things that sat alongside orders for heating coils and staff memos in my inbox.

This letter, however, was purposeful. It had taken time.

I switched on the cabin light, inserted my car key into a small crevice in the sealed envelope and neatly tore it open. The response was typed on a white card, purposefully marked 'From the desk of His Excellency Robert Gabriel Mugabe' in flowing cursive script that was elegant yet understated. He had learnt much from his exile in London.

Dear Mr Smith,

Mr and Mrs Mugabe thankfully acknowledge the receipt of your invitation. They apologise for the delay in responding and further take this opportunity to respond to your invitation in the affirmative.

Yours sincerely,
Jabulani Mkandua
Secretary
PS: Please be advised that Mr Mugabe is a vegetarian of long standing.

An African grey

It was a violent sound, subtle but nonetheless violent. Familiar too. Mauve jacaranda blooms being crushed by the hundreds. Spring buds exploding purple on the tar. Pauline listened intently to the melancholy sound as Johan's dilapidated Jetta made its way through the suburb of Proclamation Hill, a neighbourhood built on a gentle rise overlooking a vast industrial sprawl. A pair of concrete cooling towers dominated the skyline outside her window. The rush of air coming through the passenger window soothed her unsettled thoughts. She had never known spring to be this miserable.

Johan switched the radio on. She felt distant from the laughter it introduced, continued to stare at the washed-out pallor of spring that surrounded her. Like rot, she thought, a spreading fungus, her glance taking in the familiar and discoloured koppie where the Iscor factory was located. The smokestacks ruined everything – even the failed radiance of the jacaranda trees. It was no wonder Sunette had been so desperate to get out.

Pauline tried not to think of her daughter; she would see her in less than an hour. The car picked up speed. Pauline rolled up her window. Charley, Johan's parrot, made a squawking sound, then resumed nibbling on his treat in the back seat. Why did Johan have to bring the bird with them? Charley was the cause of all of this shit in the first place. Looking at the Voortrekker Monument on her left, its sandstone form resolute if nothing else, the feeling sneaked upon her again; she had never known spring to be this miserable.

A FOREIGN SPRING. She thought the headline on page three of today's *Pretoria News* summed up things pretty well. The article, in the weekend focus section, told how the city's government – blacks – had ordered that no new jacaranda trees be planted. The decree was aimed to fall in line with new environmental legislation aiming to stop the spread of alien plant species in South Africa.

'Jacarandas are not a local tree species,' the article read. 'They were first imported from Argentina by Mr J.A. Cilliers in 1888.' Maybe that's where that old street name came from, Cilliers Street, she had thought. She was also unsure of the point of the photograph illustrating the story. It depicted a heavyset old jacaranda. Tacked onto the stem was a plastic advertising board with a telephone number, and the words, Need to Loose Weight? According to the caption, the tree was in Walker Street, Brooklyn. It said nothing about the spelling error.

Johan fiddled with the tuner, erasing the young black voice that had started reading the news. The parrot issued a garbled squawk at the loud static. Johan settled for a music station.

'What time did they say they would be there?' Johan asked. He was in a dark mood.

'At one.'

'Shit, we'll have to move it.'

Sunette had suggested they meet at BJ's, a chain restaurant perched over the N1 highway in Midrand. Neutral territory. Since the blow-up Marten had sworn never to visit his in-laws in Pretoria again, had even gone so far as to forbid both of them from visiting their daughter's marriage home in Johannesburg.

Sunette had met Marten in France, in the transit area at Charles de Gaulle. The twenty-one-year-old had been on her way home from Rotterdam after a two-year stint as a nanny, the shyly confident economics doctorate on his way to a conference in New York. After trading polite conversation in a queue at the duty-free, Marten had suggested a cappuccino. Three months later, after a flood of email traffic, he visited Pretoria.

He wasn't much to look at, Pauline decided when they collected him from the airport. He had bad teeth and his lanky frame was in need of a tan. His fashion sense was peculiar too: a brown corduroy jacket with jeans and pale yellow moccasins. No, she didn't think much of him at all as Johan's car had pulled into the drive of their redbrick Iscor house in Proclamation Hill.

Johan helped with the baggage. The visitor would stay in the spare room, the one where Johan's mother had spent her last years, prone on her back, waiting for the muslin gloom to seize her. Finally, it did. As they showed the visitor into the room, Pauline saw that Florence had taken a gilt-framed photograph of Sunette in her matric dance dress from the lounge and placed it on the bedside table. She would have to speak to the bent old domestic. First the milk and sugar, now this.

Dinner that evening did not go well. Marten said he didn't eat red meat, which posed a problem. Florence had taken chops out of the deep freeze. When Johan offered to shoot down the road and get something from Kentucky, Marten had politely refused, said he would be happy with salad. All through dinner, which they ate on trays in the lounge, Pauline had watched the young man's wandering eye, the details it took in: Johan's long-service certificate next to the family photographs on the wall; the indoor ferns; the sandstone head of an old-timer and bronzed kudu statuette, both from the Kruger Park; Charley's cage, the worn carpet surrounding it covered with newspaper. But this had been long before the blooms, or the blow-up, even before the strange visitor from abroad asked Johan if he could marry his stepdaughter.

The Jetta was sluggish and the other cars seemed to fly by in the faster lanes. Pauline looked at the animals feeding at a green trough in the grounds of the new mint alongside the highway. It was a bizarre mix: a gaggle of white ducks and a lone blesbok, some ostriches too. A stern electric fence was all that kept them from wandering onto the busy highway. It all seemed so contrived, awkward, a fact shown up by the muddy brown water gushing out of an artificial fountain. It had recently stormed, the first rains of the season.

The radio continued to fill the silence in the car. Even the parrot was uncharacteristically quiet. Charley, a male Congo African grey, was a gift from a retrenched co-worker of Johan's. The ironworks had cut back on staff, Johan included. While

Pauline was at work every day, and Florence sat out on the frostbitten lawn talking with neighbouring domestics, Johan had patiently made friends with the bedraggled bird, teaching it new words.

He started out with simple greetings, but when the bird unexpectedly imitated a regular expression – 'Florence, answer the fucking telephone!' – Johan started experimenting. 'Hello, I'm Vuyo Mbuli' and 'Tshwane *se moer*' always generated a laugh from visitors. The parrot, which had been practically bald when he was given to Johan, also stopped stripping his tiny body of its plumage. As winter passed, and a mauve epiphany swept across the city, the parrot began to sprout a fresh new growth of feathers in a distinctive blend of smoky white and cigarette-ash grey. All through the seasonal summer rains, Johan searched for work, although mostly he sat on the couch at home. At length the autumnal jacaranda trees shed new gifts: mussel-shaped seed pods. In parliament, a bill regarding invasive alien plant forms was passed. Johan continued to look for work.

How little things had changed, Pauline thought. Johan remained unemployable, and the jacaranda trees were on autopilot, the recently bare branches radiant with a profusion of fresh purple blooms.

'No, not this one,' she said. Johan had indicated to turn off at the Shell Ultra City. 'It's at the next one, Caltex.' Johan veered back onto the highway, the car behind hooting angrily.

It seemed stupid that things had been reduced to this. If it hadn't been for the damned parrot things would have been different, Pauline told herself; ordinary. Ordinary was nice.

She blamed the blasted parrot for everything, and Johan.

After the wedding, the newlyweds had visited her every Sunday, driving all the way out from Johannesburg. Admittedly these meetings had been hard for Marten, Johan disregarding the recently employed investment banker in favour of television while mother and daughter chatted. Once, in a rare moment, Pauline apologised for Johan's manner, even managing a nostalgic laugh about her former life in Piet Retief, before Johan, with Sunette's real father. But then the parrot spoiled everything.

It all happened on an unexceptional Sunday, shortly after New Year. Sunette was excitedly describing the house they had just made an offer to buy in Parkhurst. Sensing that he was not a part of the animated conversation, Charley cocked his flat, broad head and announced himself.

'Mandela is 'n houtkop. Mandela is 'n houtkop.'

Johan simply chuckled.

'Mandela is 'n houtkop.'

'Is that really necessary?' Marten asked.

Johan released a low, throaty rumble. Sensing the start of something, Sunette asked Marten to show her mother his new company car, a silver Mercedes.

'Mandela is 'n houtkop,' Charley continued. The awkward, tongue-tied parcel of speech pitched itself squarely into the late morning silence.

'Are you proud of your latest accomplishment?' Marten evenly stated. 'Excuse me if I have missed the humour in it.'

Pauline laughed confusedly. She hadn't heard this latest one.

'*Mandela is 'n houtkop.*'

'Come on, shut him up, Johan,' Sunette pleaded sternly.

'Don't bother, we're leaving.' Marten stood up from his seat. 'Your stepfather's a lunatic.'

'What?'

'You heard me.'

'Well at least I don't come from a country that was fucked up by the Germans in two days.'

'*Net so,*' Pauline interjected.

'What the hell do you mean by that?'

'We checked in the encyclopaedia. Hitler fucked your country up in just two days. Two days!'

'*Heil Hitler! Heil Hitler!*'

'You tell him, Charley, you tell him,' Johan roared.

'Jesus,' Marten exclaimed. 'Your pettiness has reached new levels of stupidity, Johan. Do you really understand what you are teaching that bird? Can your small mind even begin to understand what Hitler did?'

'Yes, yes. Just because you're a doctor who drives a fancy car, what the hell makes you so grand? Hitler fucked your country up in two days, man.'

Pauline recalled Johan wiping tears of laughter from his eyes as he delivered these words.

'It's time to go, Sunette.' Looking angrily at the pugnacious man seated on the couch, Marten slipped in an unconscious afterthought, '… back to civilisation.'

'What?' Johan blurted, jerking himself upright in his chair.

'Yes, you heard me, back to civilisation.' He was more certain about his statement the second time. 'This fucking house is caught in a time warp. You people live in the past. Wake up!'

'Marten, leave it,' Sunette had chided him softly.

'*Heil Hitler!*'

'*Sê vir hom, Charley*,' Johan stated. He flashed a conceited smile.

'Fine. If that's how you feel about things, but let me just tell you one thing.' Marten trembled. 'God is a fuck-up! A fuck-up! Why else would he create the likes of you?' He stammered the last of his words.

With unexpected alacrity Johan had leapt from his chair, grabbing Marten by the throat.

'Come on, say that again, I dare you.'

Pauline still remembered the eerie morning silence that followed, the peculiarity of the freeze-framed details as time stood momentarily still. The parrot's chant. Sunette's smile, a timeless smile, one that could never be erased from the school photograph – Florence had returned it to the mantelpiece. Outside, a Sunday church bell rang out above the fading burgundy roofs of the houses on Proclamation Hill, and a passing car spluttered and backfired. Inside Sunette's womb, a month-old secret kicked.

Johan steered the car into a parking place. A sunburnt man with a green security bib waved them in. He had a dejected look. Pauline saw an old tog bag concealed under a bench nearby. Probably his. Johan waved him off gruffly. It had taken a week of nightly arguing to get her husband to agree to come to Midrand, to finally get to the entrance of BJ's so that she could see her grandson. It would be their first meeting since the row.

They were waiting at a four-seater table overlooking the highway. Pauline waved and ran to meet her daughter. By the time Johan reached the table she was already cooing over the small bundle wrapped up in a carrycot.

'Congratulations,' he stated without lessening his stride. He was holding Charley against his chest. Pauline chased after him, followed him to the empty bar counter in the middle of the restaurant.

'What the hell are you doing?'

'Just the sight of him makes me sick.' He placed the bird on the counter and climbed up onto a barstool.

'Don't you want to see your grandson?'

'Not if that moegoe has to be here.'

'That moegoe is a part of our family now, whether we like it or not.' The words slipped out unexpectedly.

'Okay, I see how it is now.'

'Ag, suit yourself then.' Pauline returned to her daughter.

The weight of the young child was strangely familiar in her arms. It reminded her of long ago, picnics at the dam in Piet Retief, another life. She concentrated on the bundle in her arms. Her grandson had definitely inherited his father's looks although she could see hints of Sunette, slight, but nonetheless distinct. They discussed the shortlist of possible first names: Anton, Eugene or Hugo. When Marten joked about his son's rubicund cheeks, they all laughed.

'These are for you,' Marten stated, handing Pauline an envelope. The photographs showed Sunette in a hospital bed. Included in the small selection was a picture of Marten's mother, beaming and holding the newborn in her arms. Pauline recognised the roses in the background; she had sent them.

Marten ordered lunch, his insistence that Pauline stay polite but firm. Every so often during the meal she looked over to Johan. He appeared to be staring at nothing. Julia Roberts danced on a television screen above his head.

As the young waitress removed their finished meal, Pauline's cellphone suddenly rang.

'Come on, let's go.' Johan was walking towards the table. He craned his head over the carrycot as he stopped at the table. He looked at Sunette.

'Congratulations, young lady.' He promptly walked off.

Pauline wanted to apologise but simply started crying. Sunette held her in a long embrace as she stood to leave. It felt definitive, like they would never meet again.

'I wonder why they built that restaurant to face south,' Johan mused as the Jetta slowly accelerated down the on-ramp. 'Surely it must be cold in winter.'

Pauline said nothing.

As they passed the mint, he spoke again.

'So how is the little fellow?'

'The doctor says he's fine, nothing wrong with him at all. Ag Johan, he's so cute. He reminds me of Sunette when she was a baby.'

'I'm happy for her, although I still don't like that foreigner, not one bit.'

'Can't you leave it now?'

'Not after what he said, fucking Hollander.'

'*Heil Hitler!*' Charley was seated on the driver's chair behind Johan's head.

'Tell the bird to shut up, Johan. He's caused enough shit as it is.'

'Don't get all soft on him just because of the baby. That bloody Hollander still owes us an apology.'

'*Heil Hitler!*'

'Shuddup Charley,' Pauline shouted. 'Just shuddup!'

Pauline folded forward, sobbing quietly into her lap. She had been crying so much of late.

'*Heil Hitler!*'

'*Voertsek*,' Johan yelled, lashing out at the bird behind him. The bird defensively attacked, biting him on his neck before retreating in a flutter to the rear of the car.

'*Eina*, shit!'

Johan licked his finger, rubbing the spittle into his wound. 'Useless fucking bird, just look what he did.'

Searching for the parrot's reflection in his rear-view mirror, Johan finally spotted him. The bird was listlessly plucking at his neat plumage.

'Stupid fucking bird.'

Pauline said nothing as she leaned her head against the window and focused on the yellow line alongside the speeding car. A yellow line was used to indicate the emergency lane, she had learnt at driving school. Surely Sunette would understand. But how would Marten react? Would he be prepared to drive out all the way from Jo'burg just because of an uncertain whim? She concentrated on the thought of leaving Johan some more. It was an uncertain thing, fragile and new, just like the purple blossoms that carpeted the road near home.

Waiting for Mister President

'What are those white poles?'

The battered Land Rover hit another indent in the road. Roy Katz bounced on his seat, his question unanswered. The man seated in front of him, Grey Kangulu, continued reading, resolute in his silence.

'Grey?'

The district hospital inspector closed the book he was reading, an East African travel biography lent to him by Roy a week into their month-long tour of hospitals and clinics in the Lilongwe region. Grey squinted at the oblique reflection of his interrogator showing in the rear-view mirror attached to the passenger door.

'What are those white poles?' Roy repeated as their eyes met in the mirror. Grey looked away, to the poles lining the sides of the dismal road leading into the Malawian capital.

'To be sure, I can't exactly say.' He dropped his head and continued reading.

Roy looked intently at the man seated in front of him, at the speckles of grey on his short-cropped head of hair. Late forties, he guessed when they were first introduced, easily a decade older than him. Taller too, and leaner, although not in the way of the sickly people he spent his days looking at through his camera's viewfinder, more like an athlete – a long-distance runner.

Grey's head bobbed as the Land Rover hit another pothole. Unperturbed, he pushed his square, gold-rimmed glasses back into place and continued reading. Roy gave up on an answer and returned to the whitewashed poles flashing by.

They had appeared overnight, although not without warning. The day before, on a late afternoon stroll to Lilongwe's city centre from his guesthouse, situated on the eastern outskirts of town, Roy had stopped to look at a series of shallow holes dug alongside the main road. Dark mounds of soil – healthy but useless – lay heaped next to the knee-deep hollows. When he asked passers-by the purpose of these shallow cavities, they would either smile bemusedly or shake their heads agitatedly: they didn't know.

The driver slowed to avoid another waterlogged pothole, the braking followed by a familiar jolt. Roy stuck his head out of the window. The sharpness of the afternoon sun momentarily blinded him. It was midsummer, the rainy season; a muggy heat clung to his back. Looking down at the road, he saw that the thunderstorms, which always came drifting in over the grassy plains to the east, had created deep furrows along the road's edge.

He felt there was something quite familiar about this view now, of the main road with its pockmarked surfaces and dangerous verges. Every afternoon when he returned he would stroll alongside it, to and from town, past barricaded private residences, a military stockade and a golf course, passing scenes both unremarkable and strange, almost like Pretoria – but not.

It was, however, the crab-like manoeuvring of the buses engaging the gradual incline out of town that fascinated him most. Despite his anticipation, the buses never collided with oncoming traffic, nor did they quite swerve off the road into the muddy channels he was staring at from the moving Land Rover. Things continued working, somehow, even the buses, which belched thick diesel smog every time they struggled up the incline to get out of town.

Yesterday, in a flurry of inspiration, he had tried, quite unsuccessfully, to photograph these black clouds, having previously been intrigued by how they effortlessly drifted over residential walls lined with jagged bits of glass. It was a whimsical idea, of course, although he nonetheless tried, setting up his large-format camera on its tripod, waiting, and then ultimately failing. In the end he settled on a photograph of one of the unexplainable holes, although it too turned out to be an unyielding subject.

Roy spotted the grassy traffic circle in the distance. He pulled his head into the cabin as the driver steered onto the kerbside, bringing the Land Rover to an abrupt stop.

'Can I buy you a beer or something?' The primly dressed health official was helping Roy to off-load his equipment.

Grey was slow to answer.

'Yes, thank you,' he replied, handing Roy the last of his camera equipment. He slammed the Land Rover's door shut.

The guesthouse was shielded from view by an imposing brick wall covered with huge palm leaves stuck vertically into the ground. To access it required a short walk along a muddy path near the grassy traffic circle down a quiet branch road. A shirtless young man in his early twenties greeted the pair as they arrived at a corrugated-iron gate. He wore a silver earring in his left ear, a gold-plated stud in his right.

'What are all those white poles in the ground for?'

'It means the president is coming,' the young man offered.

'The poles?' Roy repeated, purposely reducing his question to the barest minimum of words.

The young man shut the gate. He walked past Roy, took up a pair of rusted garden clippers leaning against the wall, looked to Grey, and shot off a rapid-fire explanation.

'They're flagpoles,' Grey translated.

'Yes, it means the president is arriving.' The young man beamed at Roy.

'When?' Roy queried.

'Soon.'

'You mean today?'

'Yes, soon.'

Grey said nothing.

A group of travellers in an overland truck had arrived just before, the garden surrounding the small colonial-style homestead at the centre of the barren yard dotted with colourful tents in various stages of construction. An elderly couple dressed in swimming costumes smiled and greeted them in a trim Dutch accent as they passed.

'They'll all be gone by tomorrow morning,' explained Roy. He pointed Grey to a chair on the stoep.

'I never knew this place even existed.' Grey seated himself, his gaze fixed on the tented camp. 'Every day I pass this place on the bus. I would never have guessed that so many people were here, sleeping out in the open like this.'

'It is very pleasant here.'

'And full.' Grey did not offer it as a joke.

'How about a beer?'

'A cold drink is fine,' responded Grey, still absorbed by the encampment of colourful, tented mushrooms in front of him. 'I don't drink alcohol,' he added as an afterthought.

Roy returned with bottled orange juice and a plastic tumbler filled with gin. They drank silently, in the morose way of familiar strangers. The evening languorously unfolded. At one point Grey smiled quizzically as their silence was interrupted by the sound of a gas burner being ignited. The smell of coffee soon followed. Outside, a bus passed. It was a beguiling lull, still in its own peculiar way, thought Roy, even if it was not quite comforting. He would be happy to see the back of it all.

Grey decisively finished off the last of his lukewarm drink. He turned to Roy. 'What music do you listen to?'

'I don't really listen to music.'

Grey replaced the empty bottle on the table.

'But surely you must listen to music?' he declared evenly. 'Everyone listens to music.'

'I suppose.' Roy paused. (What was he getting at with his question?) 'I don't really make an effort to listen, if that's what you mean, not for enjoyment. I don't own any CDs nor do I go to any shows.'

Grey looked back out at the yard. 'You must at least own a radio?'

'Yes, but mostly I listen to talk shows – if I listen at all.'

Grey nodded his head slowly, as if to make clear his comprehension of Roy's answer. He watched a man in khaki shorts and matching cap pour a thick stream of black coffee into a tin mug. It was time to go.

'I am sorry I didn't know about the poles,' Grey remarked as he approached the gate. He was insistent that he could not stay for dinner, offering no reason other than he could not stay. He swatted at a moth as they passed an electric light near the gate – it was already attracting insects.

'I only recently transferred here from Blantyre. You could say that I am still getting to know the peculiarities of our capital.' Even with this revelation his tone remained poised, aloof almost, his pronunciation exacting.

'That's okay, at least we now both know what the poles mean,' Roy answered, wondering if Grey was a product of that famous school, the one they always spoke of, the one with the white teachers from England.

'Yes, the president will be arriving soon.' With that Grey slipped past the gateman and was gone.

Roy had seen another, larger hole on his walk from town the day before. It was a much deeper hole, also situated on the main road, itself just a short distance from the traffic circle. It burrowed vertically into the ground, just like a mineshaft. There was no chevron tape to warn pedestrians of its existence, just a heaped mound of earth nearby on which people occasionally sat, waiting. Inquisitive as to its purpose, he peered into the hole. It was easily three metres deep, he reckoned, possibly an unfinished drainage device of sorts. He dropped a stone into it, briefly revelling in the childhood memory as it broke the meniscus of the water with a splash. Plop! He would have repeated the action had he not noticed the teenagers staring at him from a nearby bus stop. Faking nonchalance, he returned to the guesthouse, entirely forgetting about the encounter by dinner.

'Do you think I've missed the president?'

The question was just a subterfuge. The Land Rover was making slow progress from the Catholic mission hospital and Roy was impatient to get back, he wanted to shower. The distinctive and lingering smell of the hospital he had just visited, of burnt porridge and wood, filled his nostrils.

'I don't know,' responded Grey. 'Let me ask the driver.'

The driver's answer was short and did not need translation.

'When do you think he'll pass by, then?'

'Soon, maybe tomorrow even,' Grey translated.

'Can't he be more precise?'

'I suppose he could but then you would be forcing him to lie just to make you happy.'

Grey's cryptic response irritated Roy. In spite of their modest exchange the night before, his conversational manner had remained guarded and circumspect. Nothing had changed between them, even after the drink. He chose to remain inscrutable and distant.

The road ahead suddenly took on a familiar aspect; they were nearing the guesthouse. Roy repeated his dinner offer of the night before – it just seemed to come out. He knew Grey would in any case decline, leaving him free to spend his last evening cataloguing the various rolls of film he had shot, possibly even turn in for an early night.

'Thank you, I accept. I recommend the Lilongwe International, it serves an excellent buffet.' Grey also preferred to be seated on the terrace overlooking the hotel's manicured lawn.

Throughout dinner their dialogue was ritually polite, Grey patiently repeating answers to questions he had already fielded before, each statement of fact devoid of personal engagement in the matter. At one point, as the possibilities of their stilted exchange eased, the two found themselves in disagreement over the name of a health assistant (Winston or Dickens?) at one of the hospitals. Convinced he was correct, Roy removed his journal from the camera bag hitched over his chair behind him.

'What is that?' Grey pointed to a photograph pasted into the book.

'A Polaroid. I keep them so that I don't get mixed up about who said what when I'm back home.'

Grey reached across the table and seized the journal. He removed his gold-rimmed glasses from his shirt pocket. They always gave him the appearance of a stern, middle-aged schoolmaster, Roy thought. Quietly, patiently, very deliberately, he viewed each picture in the weathered journal. He repeated the process twice.

'I do not like this picture.' He handed Roy his journal, open on a page containing a single picture.

Grey pressed his finger down on the face of a naked woman, her limp breasts mere appendages to a wrinkled and emaciated body. It was the starkest image in his series. All his other photographs merely buttressed this one, none of them rivalling the expressionless death face worn by the young woman.

'I do not like it, not at all.' His tone was even and steadfast.

'I am not sure what you mean. Do you mean the picture itself or what it shows?'

'Both, everything,' Grey replied, withdrawing his hand to take another measured sip of his drink.

Roy looked down at the photo. Grey's smudged fingerprint could not erase the impact of the young woman's penetrating stare, which directly confronted the camera. Seated directly behind her, propping her up for the photograph was an elderly woman. She wore a pink dress with a purple floral pattern.

'I can't help what I photograph, Grey.'

He said nothing, simply removed his glasses, methodically wiping them with a hanky before replacing them into his shirt pocket. With resigned patience Roy watched as Grey wiped his face, then the back of his neck.

'What do you know about that woman?' he asked when his grooming ritual was complete.

'What do you mean?'

'I mean, what do you know about that woman?'

'Um, hang on, I keep notes for all my pictures.' Roy reached for his journal. 'Here we go. Olivia Chitope, 30, with her guardian Chipila Muyare, 54, Bottom Hospital, Lilongwe, Malawi.'

'The science of saying nothing.'

Adam looked up at Grey. The gin, the heat, the cumulative effect of his busy workload; the evening unexpectedly weighed heavily on him. He emptied the last pieces of ice from the glass tumbler into his mouth, savouring the bitter taste of the local ice. He was too weary to pursue the argument he was being drawn into.

'I don't want to argue with you, Grey.' He shrugged his shoulders, smiling ruefully.

'That's not what I am proposing. All I want to know is what do you know about this woman?'

Roy looked down at the journal resting on the hotel linen. Literally speaking, the answer to Grey's question was right there, written in black pen and an untidy cursive script. But that was if his dinner guest was being literal. He was never quite sure where Grey was coming from, less so now than ever. He looked up at the district hospital inspector, then back down to his notes again. Without prompting he began to read.

'Olivia is a farmer. She was admitted to the Mithundu district hospital with TB and later referred to Lilongwe. Chipila is her aunt. Olivia's husband left her after discovering she had TB. He has subsequently remarried. Olivia has three children, and also mentioned a stillborn child. Although she claims that there is no history of TB in the family, further questioning revealed that her mother, Chipila's sister, died from TB – "a long time ago". Despite the physical discomfort she continually speaks about, Olivia says she is mentally okay. Asked what her chances of pulling through are, a duty nurse replied: "Not so good."'

Roy closed his journal.

'So it is settled, then, you know something about her.' There was no malice or sarcasm about his statement, just the same steady register. 'Now you can tell your magazine readers something instead of nothing about this country.' He promptly stood up and marched off in the direction of the buffet table for dessert.

They ate in silence. Roy ordered another double gin, Grey coffee. There were intervals when Roy wanted to speak. How long had Grey been married to his wife? What was his eldest daughter's name, the one at university? Questions formulated around small fragments Grey had let slip while they were on their trips, anecdotes without detail. He also wanted to ask if he had ever lived abroad. Roy particularly wanted to ask this question. Grey knew far more than he sometimes let on. But he said nothing, silence being easier.

He gulped down his gin, ordering another soon after.

On the stairs outside the hotel, he moved drunkenly to shake hands with the tall district hospital inspector. Grey smiled, his hands firmly held against his sides.

'Prowlers,' he stated concisely, seizing Roy's arm firmly. 'You have to be careful out there in the dark. It is late, and you might also get lost. Come, it's this way.'

The road leading to the guesthouse was empty now. Water had collected in the road's pitted surface and reflected a half-formed moon. Roy drunkenly wondered if it would be possible to photograph the scene. It had all the banal terror of one of Takuma Nakahira's photographs, everything dark and immanent and ordinary. He heard Grey ask him something.

'Hey?'

'I said, you must at least know Brenda Fassie,' Grey repeated, walking behind him.

'I've heard her name before but I can't say I know her music.'

'That's a great pity, although I do not personally like South African music.'

'What music do you ...'

The question yielded to gravity as Roy suddenly fell. He dropped like a stone, only heavier, faster.

The water at the bottom of the hole was cold and left a muddy aftertaste in his mouth when he stood upright. As he steadied himself he felt his feet sag into the thick, viscous mud at the bottom. Instinctively, he clawed at the sides of the hole, aware too that something clung to his neck. He grabbed at it, falling backwards. It was simply a discarded plastic bag.

Roy stood himself upright again, the water measuring just below his navel. It had cushioned his fall. He reached down into it, feeling at his legs. Nothing broken, nothing hurt.

'My cameras!' The thought and the utterance happened all at once.

He bent down onto his knees, frantically searching the silted muck with fanned-out fingers.

'Mr Katz, are you okay?'

Something about the formality of Grey's address made Roy pause. He looked up at the silhouette above him.

'My cameras, I can't find my fucking cameras.'

He heard Grey chuckle.

'Fuck you, man! There isn't anything funny about this.'

'I agree, Mr Katz, there isn't.'

Grey held out something indistinct over the hole – Roy's camera bag.

'I see you forgot that I was carrying your bag.'

'Oh Jesus, thank God.'

'I wouldn't mind if you thanked me too. Your equipment is very heavy.'

Roy laughed, polite at first, then incrementally louder, his outpouring suddenly given over to a mad frenzy of thrashing. He sobbed drunkenly. Grey silently watched from above.

'I'm sorry,' Roy offered as he composed himself.

'I think it's been a difficult few weeks for you.'

'I don't know what I feel about the past few weeks.'

'I'm sure you'll have plenty of time to think about that once we get you out of this hole.'

Roy followed Grey's advice and tried to pull himself up. It was hopeless, each time he simply fell back into the water.

'You're going to have to get a ladder or a rope at the guesthouse,' Roy panted.

Grey retreated, leaving Roy standing motionless in the dark hole. He listened to the night, stared intently at the sky overhead. But for a thin smudge of white cloud cover it was a perfect night, stars everywhere. He stared intently at the constellation of light above him. He couldn't name any of the stars he was looking at.

'The guard won't let me in.' Grey breathed heavily.

'What?'

'He says he won't let me in.'

'But for fuck's sake, he knows who you are?'

'It is not the same young man we met yesterday.'

'But can't you explain to this other guy what happened?'

'I did.'

'And what did he say?'

'He refused.'

'Didn't you ask him to call the owners of the guesthouse?'

'I did.'

'And he refused?'

'Yes.'

'Fuck!' Roy smashed a fist into a dark wall of stone and earth. It hurt.

'At least Olivia and the others are safe up here with me,' Grey remarked, now seated on his haunches.

'Thank God for that.' Roy leaned himself against the side of the hole. It was cool.

'You seem to thank God for many things, Mr Katz.'

Roy smiled. He could just as easily have told the lanky bureaucrat to fuck off, but he didn't. He looked up.

'Grey, have you ever lived in another country, I mean outside of Africa?'

'Why do you ask?'

'It's just the way you speak about certain things.'

'Manchester, England. I completed a postgraduate diploma in tropical medicines there.'

'How was it?'

'Unfamiliar.'

'Is that all?'

'I am using one word to say many things.'

'Why unfamiliar?'

Grey paced around the circumference of the hole. He stopped.

'Let's just say that the music over there is rather peculiar if not quite strange.'

'Strange, how?'

Grey remained quiet. It was one of those resolute silences of his. Nothing would be forthcoming, Roy knew that and he slowly declined his head. There would be no more talk, or at least nothing other than was functionally necessary to get him out of the hole.

'Do you dislike me, Grey?'

'Why would I dislike you?'

'You keep calling me Mr Katz.'

'It is your name, is it not?'

'Yes, I suppose it is.'

Grey continued to pace the circumference of the hole. He suddenly switched direction.

'I just find it strange that you don't like music, that's all. Maybe that is why your wife left you.'

The remark was unexpected. Not only did it suggest that Grey noted every word he had said, even when speaking to others, it also hinted at an unexpected level of empathy from the man. But how did he come to connect the two: Kirsten and his apparent disregard for music?

'I don't think it has anything to do with you!'

'I'm sorry, you're quite right. It is your personal business.'

Grey paused, sneezed, resumed pacing the hole and started speaking again. 'I have been thinking. I have a friend in the health department who lives nearby, I am sure he will be able to help us with some rope or a ladder.' At that, Grey disappeared into the night.

Roy felt utterly exhausted. He had cut his arm during the fall and it throbbed somewhat painfully now. Looking up, he listened to the sound of an approaching car. His expectant emotion was dashed, the car passing by at speed. It was the same with the pedestrians: an approach of voices (hopefully Grey's), the crispness of an unfamiliar lexicon, laughter (occasionally), then silence. Leaning against the vertical rise of the hole, a slight tremor of cold and fear now running through his body, he listened to the silence, imperfect as it was. Insects chirped. Occasionally, in the far distance, a dog would bark. He even thought he heard the sound of a child crying. Nothing, though, to suggest Grey's return.

He wondered if the incomprehensible man had simply decided to leave him there. He had behaved badly at dinner, drinking too much. He again considered the possibility that Grey had simply abandoned him. It was a possibility, albeit remote given Grey's character. Presuming then that he was returning, how long would he still have to wait? And what if it started raining, which it was likely to do? He snorted. Finally he understood what all those stern warnings at school had been about.

Like most of his classmates back then, he had grown up in one of those half-formulated suburbs on the periphery of Pretoria, where rain-filled foundations and open stormwater drains possessed a special kind of wonder. The falling stone, dropped into the hole three days before, had reminded him of this. He checked the thought, resolving also to call out to the next passer-by.

The silence congealed, the night becoming thick. Roy found himself drawn back to his conversation with Grey at dinner. Why had the picture upset Grey so much? It was merely a declaratory statement of what they had both seen, nothing more. He tried to recall the encounter frozen in the image. Nothing. Without the aid of his journal he wasn't even sure he could remember the woman's name, not even that.

A car approached, a snatch of music audible as it passed by.

Why was Grey so persistent about knowing what music he liked? Could the old stiff not see that he was simply pulling his leg, of course he liked music. Nina Simone's 'Monster', 'Blind Love' by Tom Waits; he listened to a lot of music.

'How does it feel to treat me like you do? When you've laid your hands upon me, and told me who you are.'

The song rang clear in his head, seemingly sneaking out of nowhere. It was New Order's 'Blue Monday', a favourite. Sombre, deadpan vocals delivered over a staccato dance beat; in its totality, the song was the purest (or did he simply mean most modern?) description of being happy and sad at the same time.

He tensed.

'Grey?' He did not want to sound too urgent. 'Grey!'

Nothing, just a stiff neck and a sky filled with nameless stars.

'Tell me how does it feel when your heart grows cold?'

Thinking about it now, here, three or more metres underground, far from Johannesburg's grubby yet undeniably cosmopolitan glow, the lyrics struck him as peculiarly resonant, as if he were hearing them for the first time. To think that he had requested the song at his wedding, that everyone had danced to it.

'Tell me how does it feel when your heart grows cold?' The song kept repeating itself in his head, reminding him of Kirsten.

There was no definite date on which it happened, not as far as he could remember, just the clear knowledge afterwards of having *been* in love, of not *being* in love anymore. The difference between the two was more than just semantic, so much so that now, five years after their divorce, Kirsten still refused to speak to him, the silence between them leaving him free to pursue, camera in hand, a failing wanderlust.

He stood upright and attentive as he heard the muffled sound. It was a siren, which was pointedly odd. The ambulances at the various hospitals he had visited were barely functioning hand-me-downs. Perhaps Grey had gone straight to the nearest police station. It did seem rather over the top, but then Grey was both unpredictable and without subtlety, all formality in fact. A faint hint of blue flashed dimly overhead, the sound of the accompanying siren growing louder until it seemed to fill the entire cavity in which he stood trapped.

Roy waited for the sound of braking, of car tyres screeching, the commotion of voices it would herald – none of which happened. The siren passed, together with the accompanying blue flashing light and an unseen entourage of cars. A still calm settled over the road and its environs.

A dog barked somewhere. Insects, hidden beneath bushes or sitting high up in trees, trilled in the night. Far above all of this, stars continued to burn with the intensity of suns. Defeated, Roy slumped heavily against the cold wall of the hole, causing bits of dislodged stone and earth to tumble into the water. Plop! Plop. He was trapped, he realised, looking down at the half-moon haphazardly reflected off the water's rippled surface. There was nothing he could do. Patiently, Roy Katz waited for Grey Kangulu's eventual return.

A gift of stones

I

The taxi turned and sped off along the embankment towards the city. I looked down at the group of protesters congregated near the river's edge. They were laughing, their anti-dam placards lazily resting against iceboxes and picnic baskets. Children played in groups. Smoke drifted off the barbecue. I made my way down a slip road to a gravel parking lot. It was filled with station wagons and family sedans. I searched the crowd. It didn't take long to spot her; she was the only other Westerner in the crowd.

'Hi, Richard Cope. You must be Catherine Orton.' I thrust my hand forward.

'Oh hello, I've been expecting you,' she shouted above the youthful racket that surrounded her.

'Sorry, the ferry from Osaka was delayed. It was also a bit of an effort explaining to the taxi driver where I wanted to go. My Japanese isn't all that good.'

'All in a day's work,' Catherine tittered, her hand resting on the head of a boy wearing a baseball cap.

'Can I offer you a drink? Tea, juice, a beer?'

'Coke please, I'm not much of a fan of the local iced tea. It's rather bitter.'

'Me neither. Anyhow, follow me.'

Dressed in a sleeveless dress, Catherine's shoulder-length crop of hair waved freely in the midday breeze. Something about the colour of her dress held my attention. A new editor on the paper in London, an American, had complained about the 'restricted use of vivid prose' in my news features. As a useful bit of practice, he had suggested I work on my description things, colours for instance. It proved to be uncannily difficult. Gunmetal grey or ashen silver? I couldn't decide which of the two best described her fashionable dress.

Sitting in the back seat of the black taxi earlier, I had experienced a similar defeat. Following a route that started at the mouth of the Yoshino River, the taxi had wound its way through a dull monotony of prefabricated housing alongside the river. I tried to contain what I saw by writing a haphazard list of words and colours into my notebook: linear, temporary, grey asbestos, humid, olive, forest green, lime. My mood had lifted as we made our way further out of the glum port city of Tokushima, on the southwestern edge of Shikoku Island. The strange rural landscape impressed me with its generosity of colours, the taxi depositing me on an embankment overlooking its local celebrants.

She led me to a table where a group of women wearing floral sunhats had congregated. They bowed excitedly after she introduced me: Richard from London.

'So why the interest in covering this little meeting here

today?' she asked, handing me a polystyrene cup.

'A colleague took sick at the Tokyo office and I was seconded here from London for three months. One of my pet topics is dams.'

'Dear me, that sounds a bit dull, if you'll pardon my honesty.'

'Not at all, I suppose it does sound rather dull. I should probably explain myself better, though. I studied economics and journalism; my specialisation is public works projects and rural development. Admittedly, it's not quite *News of the World* stuff but some of us have to earn a living.'

'Where did you study?' she asked.

'Westminster Uni. You?'

'Norwich.'

'Oh, Norfolk. It's nice up there.'

'I suppose, although I thought it was remarkably crap.'

'Why?'

'Hmm, I think maybe you should ask another question, Mr Journalist.'

'Is it okay to ask what you studied?'

'Law.'

'And when did you finish?'

'Three years ago.'

She must have been about twenty-four. Six years younger than me. I took a sip on the Coke. It left a sticky aftertaste in my mouth.

'Well, aren't we a pair: a soon-to-be lawyer and a journalist who writes about developmental economics. I couldn't imagine anything more dull.'

'Speak for yourself, Jack!'

Just then I felt someone tugging at my leg. It was the young boy in the baseball cap. He wrapped one hand around my leg, holding up a stone to me with his other.

'What's he saying?'

'He wants you to take it.'

I extended an open hand. The boy carefully placed the smooth, oval stone into it, offering a garbled selection of words with it. He turned and disappeared into a thicket of adult legs.

'What did he say?'

'Nothing really, he just wanted you to have the stone.'

'A stone?' I smirked. 'Not much of a gift, is it?'

'Actually, they're quite famous around here, not worth much but nonetheless famous.'

'Do they have a name?'

'*Awa no ao-ishii.*'

'You're going to have to repeat that.'

She repeated the name, her lips pouted as she formed each of the word's component elements with her mouth. Just like a teacher, I thought, absorbed by the detail.

'*Ao* means blue, *ao-ishi* meaning blue stone.'

'They look more green than blue to me.'

'Well, smart alec, the Chinese character for blue can also mean green. For what it's worth I personally think they look sort of slate grey.'

She spoke these last words almost mockingly, her glance sideways hiding a cheeky smile. She seemed to be flirting too, if that was the right word to describe what we were doing.

I dabbed my tongue on the stone's surface. It was tasteless, and even with my spittle darkening a part of its surface, it still looked green to me.

'So why are they important?' I asked.

'Now you're asking a question. You'll have to ask Mr Himeno to explain.'

I took out my notebook.

'How do you spell that name again?'

She patiently repeated the letters, laughed when I tried to pronounce it.

'Can you write the Chinese character?' I asked. 'I mean into my notebook, please.'

She held out her hands. I watched as she practised the ideogram's strokes above the blank page before inscribing it with an unhindered flourish.

'That's quite impressive,' I said.

'Don't be fooled, it's one of the first kanji you learn when you study Japanese.'

'That doesn't make it any less impressive.'

'I'll take that as a compliment, thank you. I've been wondering, though. Where's your accent from? It's not quite your standard Home Counties version.'

'Cape Town.'

'Oh, really,' she remarked, her voice lilting. 'I've been reading a lot about it lately. Sounds like a top place.'

'I suppose, although I am not the best judge of that anymore. I left there when I finished school.'

'With your parents?'

'No, they still live there. I go visit them once a year.'

'Jammy sod.'

'Where are you from then?'

'Redcar.'

'Where?'

'Exactly,' she smiled, gathering her hair into a ponytail. Her vest pulled tightly across the contour of her breasts. She caught me looking at the crease in her fabric as it traced the outlines of her nipples, simply smiled – knowingly, I embarrassedly thought.

'I take it you're not a fan of English horse-racing, then.'

'Sorry, now I'm totally lost.'

'Oh never mind, you'll get it one day,' she laughed. 'It's near Middlesbrough. Anyway, enough of that, let's go meet Mr Himeno.'

Tsuyoshi Himeno, the leader of the anti-dam campaign, was a stout man with a neat, symmetrical crop of grey hair. He looked nothing like the beleaguered men in suits I ritually shared train rides with to Shinjuku station, in Tokyo. Instead, he had the appearance of a self-made man, of someone who regularly played golf. I put this observation down to his neat dress, a yellow Lacoste shirt primly tucked into stylish flannels.

'It's nice to meet you,' he said, confidently taking my hand. He wore an expensive watch, and his handshake was firm. His broad smile seemed to reveal his only flaw, a ropy dental job. Mr Himeno motioned me towards the barbecue, his hand pushing into the small of my back.

'Let's share some food together. Ms Catherine, please get Mr Richard Cope a beer.'

As we made our way towards the barbecue, I thought about the protesters I had recently interviewed in Uganda. Somehow, I had expected Mr Himeno to look different, more impoverished, maybe not quite like the villagers at the early beginnings of the Nile, but then also not quite like this, like that famous Japanese golfer, Jumbo Ozaki.

As it turned out, Mr Himeno's English was also impeccable. This disappointed me. Our initial introduction had been facilitated by a professor of public works theory at Hosei University, in Tokyo, the actual appointment handled by a secretary at my Tokyo office. According to her, I was simply to arrive at the scheduled location and look out for an expatriate English teacher, from the local high school. She would smooth the progress of the rest, which, in the end, simply meant replacing my Coke with a cold beer.

'Did you fly to Tokushima, Mr Cope?' I was looking towards the river when Mr Himeno asked his question; she was standing there.

'Um, no, and please call me Richard. I took the Shinkansen to Osaka, yesterday. I came over with the ferry this morning.'

'Wow,' Mr Himeno blurted, his accent marked by a distinctive American twang. 'Such a long journey, you must be very exhausted.'

'No, no, I'm fine, thank you. Just a little hot.'

'Well, please, have a relaxing time with us. We can discuss the *daijuzeki* later.'

'I beg your pardon?'

Mr Himeno laughed.

'Your Japanese is not so good, hey. The *daijuzeki* is the reason you are here today. It is the name of that old dam wall you see over there.'

He pointed in the direction of a craggy outcrop of cement that spanned the width of the river. Groups of picnickers and protesters – it was hard to distinguish them from one another – played in the shallows beneath it, children skipping past bits of plastic junk and debris as they chased after tiny fish with their nets. Clever, I thought, looking at the cement barrier near where Catherine stood, a very simple double-step design.

'It was built 250 years ago,' Mr Himeno remarked. 'At first it was just a collection of stones, almost exactly like the one you have in your hand, except much bigger, of course.'

I had forgotten about the stone. Holding it up between my fingers, all I saw was a confusing ideogram. Was it blue or green? How the hell could one word describe two colours? I put the stone in my shirt pocket.

'So is this where they want to build the new dam?' I asked.

'Sadly, yes.' His answer was earnest, almost heartfelt. 'It is a wonderful place. My father taught me how to fish here. Do you fish, Mr Richard?'

'Um, no, not anymore. I used to when I was younger, when I lived in Cape Town.'

'Cape Town? In Souse Africa?'

'Yes, I grew up there.'

'Incredible. What was your target fish?'

'I'm sorry, I don't think I quite understand what you mean by target fish?'

He looked at me perplexed.

'*Eto ne*, how would I translate that? What was your hobby fish?'

I think I got a sense of what he meant.

'Steenbras.'

'*He?* One more time, please.'

'Steenbras,' I repeated, trying to think of its more generic name. He shook his head.

'What about you, Mr Himeno, what is your, um, target fish?'

'It is not a river fish,' he sheepishly grinned. 'Do you know *ishi-dai*?' I shook my head, just as he had. We both laughed.

'Have you ever met Mandela-*san*?'

I laughed again, hoping that Mr Himeno had intended it as a joke. He gave me a quizzical look, then waved at a passer-by, a man of similar age. I could not understand anything of their conversation, just my name, which was always prefixed by that of my paper. As their exchange drew to a close, Mr Himeno looked at his watch. He grabbed at my hand.

'*Domo, domo*,' he said, shaking my hand and using an expression I knew to be one of thanks. He headed off in the direction of the marquee, erected on a gravel baseball pitch nearby. She was still standing by the river.

'What made you choose this backwater?' I asked.

'I didn't. When they replied to my application to come teach here, it was the first time I had ever heard of Tokushima. I had to check the internet to find out where it was.'

'And will you be staying another three years?'

'No, my contract expires soon, then it's back to Blighty again.'

'To Redcar?'

'No, London, if I can find a job.'

'Have you applied to many law firms?'

'Do you always ask so many questions?' she responded. 'This feels more like an interrogation than a conversation.'

'I'm sorry, I'm just curious. I mean personally.'

'Don't they warn you about getting too interested in your subjects in journalism school?'

I laughed. She had brown eyes, nothing complicated in that.

'Is it safe to walk across that thing?' I said, pointing to the concrete barrier extending across the river.

'As houses.'

'Can I walk across to the other side?'

'No, but we can walk halfway, if you want to.'

A torrent of water divided the barrier at its midpoint. I suggested that we sit on the ledge overlooking the channelled rush of water. She took her sandals off and dipped her feet into the water. Her toenails were red, I noticed, indisputably red.

'Don't you ever get lonely being out here, alone?'

'I don't know what you missed driving here this morning, Mr Defoe, but I think it is obvious I'm not alone on this island.'

'You know what I mean.'

'No, I don't.'

'I mean, isn't it difficult being a foreigner here?'

'I'm sure it is no different from when you first moved to London.'

I savoured the coolness of her retort, the verbal slap she had just given me. Somehow, I had forgotten what it was like to be challenged, to have my own brazenness chucked back at me. I was intrigued.

'Okay, peace offer.' I stood up, removed the stone from my pocket. 'Let's see how far you can throw this stone.'

'Bit macho, don't you think?'

'Come on.' I held the stone out to her.

She took the stone and looked out across the river towards the mountains framing it in the distance. Her hands were small, I saw, delicately shaped and without any jewellery. She placed the stone in her right hand and threw it. It immediately sank as it hit the water.

'I'll reserve judgement on that attempt,' I teased.

'You do that.' Her smile creased the skin across the bridge of her nose.

'I like your dress, by the way. When I first saw you I couldn't make up my mind what colour it was.'

'And what options did you come up with then?'

'I'll have to check in my notebook.'

Even though I hadn't written anything about her, I hoped this bit of flattery would help my cause. I pretended to look through the notebook. Gunmetal grey or ashen silver, I recalled from memory. I repeated these descriptions to her.

'Bit poncy, don't you think?'

'I try my best.'

'What else did you write about in there?' she unexpectedly asked.

'About you? Oh, a few things.'

'Such as?'

With her hand held up against the sun, she looked me

squarely in the eye. I suddenly and unexpectedly felt awkward, the shyness I had long since learnt to mask shining through. I flicked through my notebook, eventually pausing on a page with some preparatory scribbles from the ferry ride earlier.

'Um, let's see. Redcar. Horse races. English teacher. Single. Self-assured despite ...' I paused.

'Despite what?' she queried.

'... her circumstances.'

'Are you sure that's me you're pretending to describe?' Her contempt was palpable. With a graceful swoop she lifted up her sandals and started walking back towards the riverbank. I stumbled after her.

'I'm sorry, I was only joking. I haven't written anything about you in my notebook.'

She paused, turned and confronted me squarely. 'So you lied to me too. If I were a judge, I would tell you that you are making a terrible hash of your defence, even if your choice of words is, well, perceptive.' She smiled, and once again gathered the loosened strands of hair into a bunch.

We walked in silence to the tarpaulin shading where the press conference was due to be held. I took a seat at the rear, Catherine next to me. She whispered updates of the proceedings at uneven intervals. The softness of her voice, the momentary pleasure of her cupped hand bumping against my ear; I made no notes. In fact, I completely forgot why I had journeyed down here from Tokyo.

Mr Himeno promptly reminded me. Shortly after the press conference was over, he approached me.

'This is Mr Saito,' he stated. I shook his companion's hand.

'He is an expert on the *daijuzeki*. Come, he will teach us exactly how it works.'

I walked out along the craggy cement barrier again, only less interested in the conversation this time. My blissful interlude was over. Mr Saito spoke like a scientist and coldly tabulated the impact the proposed dam wall would have on the river's ecology. I jotted down some of his statistics, even made up for my earlier lapse with a series of earnest enquiries. Mr Himeno was impressed.

While waiting as he translated one of my questions, I saw Catherine climb into a minivan. After negotiating the slip road it followed the same meandering route as the taxi back to the city. Quite abruptly, it disappeared from view. I concentrated on the slow, unfamiliar drawl of Mr Saito. I couldn't understand a word he was saying. Patiently, I waited for Mr Himeno to translate.

Arriving at the ferry terminal an hour or so later, with Mr Himeno (he had insisted on giving me a lift), I felt a peculiarly blank sadness. It was a rather formless emotion, something unexpectedly prompted by the clipped possibilities of my encounter at the river's edge earlier. I told myself to leave it; I was getting carried away with imagined possibilities, not anything real.

'Please, a gift from Tokushima.'

Mr Himeno held out a shopping bag to me. I thanked him, insisted – a bit too forcefully, I thought afterwards on the ferry – that he not wait until I boarded. I waved him off, entered the terminal building. I sat down on a vinyl-covered chair made to look like faux marble. It was surprisingly soft, comfortable even. I peered into the bag, removing the larger gift first. It was a selection of local delicacies. I would pass them on to my colleagues at work.

The smaller package was a makeshift thing, a Burberry-pattern handkerchief neatly bound with string. It opened easily, its contents fitting snugly into the palm of my hand: two stones. They were each no bigger than quail's eggs. Accompanying them was a folded note.

A prize pair of misfits indeed, one blue, the other green.
– C.

II

'He says it looks like Soweto.'

Martin Orton was speaking to his wife, Alison.

'Ooh, it can't be as bad as that?' she chuckled.

'That's what you said, yeah!' Martin shouted to Richard from the kitchen.

'What's that?'

'I was telling Alison what you said yesterday when we passed through Skinningrove on our walk, that it looked like Soweto.'

'Do you mean that dodgy village where those men were coiling the copper wire?'

'That's the one.'

'I think so, I can't actually remember.'

'You said it looked like Soweto,' Martin repeated. Richard heard Alison laugh.

He had forgotten about the wisecrack. He might have said something like that, although he wasn't sure. He remembered that shortly after reaching the apex of Hunt Cliff, on their hike yesterday, they had passed through a desperate-looking village: Skinningrove. The local stream was a mess of rust-coloured water. Iron oxides, Martin had explained, from the old ironstone works. At some point round about then, Richard had mistakenly confused a collection of shoddy beach huts for shacks, even asked Martin whether people lived in them or not. Possibly he had said something about Soweto then. He wasn't sure.

'One or two sugars, Richard?' he heard Alison ask.

'Two, please.'

She emerged from the kitchen bearing a tray with ready-made tea on it. Richard sat up from the newspaper he had been reading on the floor.

'Thanks,' he said, sneaking a determined peek at Alison. Catherine had inherited her mother's looks, he thought, the smile, the slight bump on her nose, maybe one day the hips too.

'I'll just take one up to Cathy.'

Richard slumped back down onto his stomach again, his attention drawn to *The Guardian*'s Saturday supplement. He reached over and placed the magazine squarely in front of him. The cover showed a photograph of a plane about to collide into one of the Twin Towers in New York, probably the second. It was an image taken at the very cusp of something traumatic. He heard Catherine laugh upstairs. Martin emerged from the kitchen and sat down on the couch. He switched on the television. They were discussing the afternoon's football fixtures, the conversation interspersed with highlights from the midweek games.

'You alright there, mate?'

'No complaints, Martin, I might even go for a walk with

Cathy on the beach if her ladyship ever decides to come down.'

'I heard that!' Catherine descended the stairs. She wore a simple white T-shirt and jeans with a red cardigan slung over her shoulders. Since starting with the Japanese fashion distribution company in Farringdon, Richard had noticed how her dress sense had become looser, casual in a fastidious way. The cardigan was from Harvey Nichols.

She disappeared into the kitchen. Richard heard the fridge open. Outside, autumn was whispering. Winter fashions were already on display in the store windows in Middlesbrough. Nearer Redcar, on the road to the neighbouring coastal village of Saltburn, where they had set off on their hike the previous day, the fields were neatly cropped. The football league was also just getting started. Despite Steve McClaren's presence, Middlesbrough had gotten off to another faltering start. Martin groaned.

'What time's your train back tomorrow?' he asked.

'At five,' Catherine shouted from the kitchen.

'That means we'll have to leave here at four to get to Darlington.'

Richard opened the magazine and searched for the photo credit.

'When do you leave for China, then?' Martin asked.

He closed the magazine. China, he hadn't forgotten about his pending trip so much as put it out of his mind for their visit to Catherine's parents. He wanted to approach the assignment with a clear head next week. Unlike his previous features, which had been fitted in around his normal quota of work, his editor had specifically commissioned him to write a piece on the Three Gorges Dam, on the Yangtze River. If all went well, the story could be his big break.

'Next Thursday.'

'That soon,' Martin responded. 'Hey, Cath, you should take Rich down to the barriers by the Tees. Maybe he can find something interesting to write about that mess down there.'

Richard heard Catherine laugh.

'When do you want to go walking?' Catherine seated herself on the floor next to him, her hand resting on his back.

'We can go now if you want.'

'I'll go get a sweater for you.'

'We aren't going to be out that long, are we?'

'I thought we could go to Wetherspoons, for lunch.'

'Well in that case, can you bring my wallet down?'

'Please?'

'Please!'

The path, leading from where Catherine had grown up on an estate of neat, similar-looking bungalows, cut beneath the railway, then passed through an older neighbourhood before leading to the concrete promenade, which overlooked the beach. It was low tide, the North Sea glassy. A man dressed in a grey suit was walking his collie. The pair gingerly made their way across the pebbles and stones to the sandy stretch of beach exposed by the low tide.

It was the only part of Redcar he really liked. More so than London, which managed to perpetually reinvent itself, to stave off the legacy of the bronze men on their plinths, the landscape here was utterly exhausted. The old bridges surrounding Middlesbrough, which they had visited early yesterday morning, were museum curiosities. The harbour, he knew from subbing on the paper some years back, was largely redundant. Most of the factories were now foreign-owned too. Even the area's mythologies, if that's what he could call them, had been stolen. The illuminated night scenes, of factories lit up in electric glow, their chimneys topped with radiant blue flames, were, according to Catherine at least, the inspiration for the film *Blade Runner*. She had a thing about movies.

When Richard unexpectedly bumped into her at Oxford Circus a few months after their encounter in Japan, he suggested a drink. She counter-offered, suggesting a movie, Akira Kurosawa's *Drunken Angel*. The film was an odd choice for a first date, a desperate and rather vicious portrait of Japan after the war. Then again, it was also the type of movie one often ended up watching in London. She had stayed over at his place in Shepherd's Bush after that first night.

'Have you ever thought how important water is in our relationship?' she asked. They were walking hand in hand along the beach towards town.

'I'm not sure what you mean.' Richard was cautious in his reply. Early into their relationship, he had told Catherine that she had a capricious imagination. She hadn't spoken to him for a week afterwards, and he had subsequently learnt to better negotiate her musings.

'Well, think about it. When we first met, it was next to the Yoshino River, and then the same again in London.'

'But we met at Oxford Circus. That's quite a stroll from the Thames.'

'Yes, but remember our first date, that movie at the NFT. That's next to the Thames. And what about that nasty river outside the doctor's house in the movie, more water.'

'I think you're stretching things a bit there.'

'Do you always have to be such a dreary sod?' Catherine sighed.

She freed her hand, walked a short distance to the side and stopped. They both looked out towards the sea. The tide had exposed a treacherous reef close to the shore. Further out, the horizon was filled with the outlines of white boats, many of them large container ships, most of them headed elsewhere. They resumed walking, each silent about their thoughts. Their route eventually led them to the town centre, an unimpressive collection of gaming parlours, low-end franchises and charity shops. They walked to the pub, found a seat on the wooden deck outside.

'You should try listening to what he sings about sometime.' she said, nodding her head at the speaker. Robbie Williams was playing.

'It's hardly Sylvia Plath, is it?'

'Oh, sod off.'

Richard headed for the bar counter. Their fall-outs were becoming more routine, commonplace almost. He ordered: vodka lime for her, Guinness for him. He had probably been a bit malicious with his remark, though. The American poet had been her muse, a kindred soul whose words had reshaped the drab world outside her adolescent bedroom window, suggesting possibilities beyond the ordinariness of garden sheds and trim wooden fencing. She had even quoted the poet to him once. 'I cannot run, I am rooted.' It had been a Sunday, they were still in bed; she was explaining why she had decided to return to England from Japan.

'Ta.' He placed the drink in front of her.

'Look, I'm sorry. It's just stress, you have to understand that. You know how important this feature could be for me.'

'I know.'

'Let's try to have some fun while we're here. God knows, we could even go to Sharky's disco tonight.'

Catherine spluttered on her drink, smiled. After lunch they wandered back to the promenade. Richard bought them lemon tops, a sweet sorbet ice cream, which they ate as they walked along the route they had followed earlier. At one point, nearing the path that cut through the suburbs to her parents' home, Catherine remarked how a tall man in a mackintosh looked like his wirehaired fox terriers. They had both laughed outrageously as he passed out of earshot.

'Remember that song we were listening to the other night?' Catherine asked as their laughter subdued.

'Which one?'

'The one you said reminded you of school.'

'Oh, Soft Cell. What about it?'

'What's the name of that song when he sings that love is a dirty word?'

'I don't remember it.'

'Oh come on, of course you do.'

'No, I don't.'

'Well, anyway, that's not what I'm asking.'

'What are you asking then?'

'Do you think love is a dirty word?'

'I've never really thought about it. I'd probably say he was being a bit cynical, don't you think?'

Catherine stopped. She kneeled down, picked through a clump of stones. Taking Richard's hand, she placed one in his palm, closing his hand tightly around it. Her fingers went white from the pressure of the grip she had on his balled fist.

'Did you know that I was born just up the way from here, in Saltburn?'

'Over there, right?' Richard threw the stone in the direction of a village in the near distance.

'No, a bit further on, nearer the cliffs you walked along yesterday.'

'Why are you telling me this, Catherine?'

'I don't know, maybe it has something to do with the name. You have to admit that there is something appealing about it, the ring of those two words together: salt and burn. I like to believe that it says something about me.'

Turning, she faced Richard, paused indecisively then embraced him. It was a tight embrace.

'I wouldn't call it a dirty word either,' she whispered, 'just a difficult word. When you tell someone you love them it has implications, because that person has a hold on you. At some point it is bound to be painful.'

She started sobbing, secretly almost, then openly, loud gasping breaths of wet.

'Hey you, what's wrong?'

'Nothing,' she sniffed. 'Nothing, I'm just being silly. I think my period must be coming on.'

It was only a short walk to the house, which was quiet when they finally arrived. Martin was sitting in the kitchen, alone, drinking tea. Alison was out visiting her sister, he said, adding that Middlesbrough had drawn with Newcastle. The Saturday papers had been neatly stacked in a pile near his feet, next to the dustbin. Somewhere in all of that is the photograph of that plane, Richard thought.

'I'm off, I'll see you lot in the morning.' Martin was working the night shift.

As her father's car pulled out of the drive, and Richard sat downstairs watching television, Catherine dozed on her bed. Maybe they could walk to Saltburn in the morning and look at the hospital where she was born. Staring at the familiar geometries of the ceiling above her, she decided not. It was a stupid idea. She would tell him in London, possibly after he got back from China. After all, it's still only a pip, nothing more, just a nameless visitor. Catherine tentatively rested her hand on her stomach. A little pip, she repeated, falling asleep.

III

'Day of mist: day of tarnish' – Sylvia Plath

The laughter from earlier had stopped, the thud of bass too. The last of the partygoers hanging around the seaside disco had finally gone home. A brooding silence cloaked the Port Nolloth Hotel. Seated on a white plastic chair, Richard stared into the mist that had rolled in off the Atlantic. Nothing, he couldn't see a damn thing. He listened to the gentle lull of the ocean. Its constancy soothed his thoughts. He looked back at Catherine, sleeping in the hotel bed. She would have a hangover tomorrow. He poured the remainder of the whisky into the teacup, gulped it down. It was a feeble sedative given all that had been said earlier.

Their decision to come to Port Nolloth was the result of pure whim, decided in front of a large green signboard at an intersection on the N7. They had just exited Namibia after a week's camping. Cape Town south, Upington east, Port Nolloth west, the sign indicated. Richard had suggested they stop in Springbok, then push through to Cape Town the next morning.

Standing beneath the sign, she asked which of the three places he had never been to before. That had settled it: Port Nolloth.

He turned right at the intersection, skirting the village of Steinkopf. The Anenous Pass was unremarkable, the road thereafter straight as an arrow. It took less than an hour to shoot across the barren scrubland to Port Nolloth, at the end of the R382. Their hotel room looked directly out onto the beach, which wasn't much of an attraction. Despite the fact that it was December, midsummer, it was too cold to swim and a rasping wind occasionally blew off the ocean. Catherine had immediately jumped into the bath, leaving Richard free to stroll through the town. It was a lonely reprieve, albeit not without insight. The familiar strangeness of platteland towns intrigued him, their dull Old Mutual architecture and elevated church spires. By the time he got back, she was watching television, waiting. She was hungry too.

Catherine opted for a window seat. They could have sat anywhere; there was no one else in the restaurant.

'Not much of a menu, is it?' Richard grumbled, thinking how the place's name – Giovanni's Seafood Restaurant – should have been adequate warning.

'Oh, chill out.'

'But just look at it, we're on the West Coast and the menu reads like something from the bloody Spur.'

A waitress shyly approached their table and introduced herself.

'Hello, my name's Shaunelle. I'll be your waitress for the evening.' With a flawless smile, she deposited the menus and returned to the till.

'What kind of name is that?' whispered Catherine

'Maybe it's a contraction of Shaun and Chantal.' He spelt out the latter name in his mind. 'No, can't be. Oh hell, I haven't a clue.'

'Not much of a menu, is it?' he grumbled after reading the menu. The place's name – Giovanni's Seafood Restaurant – should have been adequate warning, he thought.

'Oh, chill out.'

'But just look at it, we're on the West Coast and the menu reads like something from the bloody Spur.'

Catherine studied the wine list at the back of the menu. 'What's that plonk your grandmother likes again?'

'Graça.'

'Oh, here it is, let's get a bottle of it.' She waved in the direction of Shaunelle.

They had already finished their first bottle by the time their meal arrived, a Giovanni's Surf 'n Turf Special, for two. As they prepared to eat, Catherine's phone beeped. It was Zoë. All through the week, she had been sending text messages from London.

'No use keeping us in suspense. Don't you want to see if she's decided to leave him or not yet?'

Catherine checked her message.

If its that horrible, just end it. ill be here when you get back. BE BRAVE. xxx

'What does she say?'

'Not much. It might snow.'

'There's a change for you.' Richard bit into a piece of pork rib.

'What do you mean?'
'The weather.'
'Oh, of course.'
'Did she say anything about her man?'
'No, she is still undecided.'
'I hope that means she'll stop texting you for a bit.'
Catherine fidgeted with her phone.
'Aren't you going to eat anything? I thought you were starving,' he asked.

Will let you know in the morning. x

During much of the meal Richard dwelt on the small and trivial details relating to his recent appointment. He had been offered a promotion, a position running the Southern Africa bureau. It was a small office, he reasoned out loud – again – but the opportunity nonetheless constituted a move up. Didn't she agree? Catherine nodded her head, even if they both knew that it was not the panacea they had hoped it would be. Their relationship was a mess of tiny fault lines and unspoken resentments. Shaunelle removed their empty plates.

'How was it, sir?'

'Oh darling, you don't have to be so formal, there's no one around,' Catherine interjected. The young waitress smiled, clearly taken by her fashionable affectations.

She asked about the silk Liberty scarf Catherine wore as a bandana. Catherine reciprocated, drawing her out on life in Port Nolloth. She was eighteen, had just finished school. After the holidays were over she hoped to study tourism in Springbok, if her father allowed. He was part owner of the restaurant and also a councillor with the district municipality.

She also liked Robbie Williams.

'Do you sell cigarettes here?'

No, she replied, but she could slip off to the café. Catherine settled for Benson & Hedges.

'I thought you quit.'

'I have, although one every so often won't hurt.'

'Please yourself.'

'Oh stop it, will you, you're like a sterile viper sometimes.'

She delivered the cigarettes on a side plate. Catherine's fringe fell across her face as she dropped her head to light a cigarette. She inhaled, coughed, took another, deeper draw.

'This isn't going to work, is it?' she said, looking down at the table.

'I don't know why you keep saying that. You called me a jammy sod when I first told you I was from Cape Town.'

'That was five years ago, Richard. Things are not as simple anymore, you know that.'

'So you keep telling me.'

Catherine waved at Shaunelle.

'The bill?'

'Oh don't be silly, darling. Bring us another bottle of wine.'

'We still have a long drive to Cape Town tomorrow.'

'You'll manage.'

He pushed over his glass of wine and asked for a new one. They drank in silence when the wine was delivered, Richard staring out of the large window at the night.

For the first time in days, Catherine looked intently at the man seated opposite her. He wasn't wearing his glasses for a change. She preferred him like that, even if she had chosen the frames. His week-old stubble was dotted with hints of grey. She had always liked to tease him about it but even these minor affections had stopped. He looked unsettled, his eyes continually darting all over the place, usually out of the window.

'When we get to Cape Town, can we go to the Mount Nelson, babes? *Vogue* says it's an absolute must.'

'Sure. Any other destinations on your list, Ms Wintour?' She smiled.

'Just the Mount Nelson, thank you.'

Maybe she would end it in Cape Town, she thought, after his parents. She lit another cigarette.

'Do you like the shirt I gave you for Christmas? I bought it at the Paul Smith shop on Ladbroke Grove,' she asked, thinking how the whole situation felt like Redcar all over again.

'Yes, it's lovely.'

'A bit of blue and bit of green.'

They both chuckled nostalgically. He looked at his watch. It was nearing eleven.

'Whatever happened to those two stones I gave you?'

'Oh, they're somewhere in a drawer in my study.'

'Close to your heart, I see.'

'In a manner of speaking.'

He wasn't sure how long the two boys had been staring at them through the restaurant's window. The shorter of the two wore a frayed brown school jersey, the other a grubby T-shirt with a faded image of the Ninja Turtles. They stared fixedly at the couple. After making a series of comical facial gestures, the taller one pointed at his stomach, then, with his fingers gathered, motioned at his mouth. He wanted food.

'God, they look starved,' Catherine remarked. She reached for her bag.

'Don't give them anything, you'll just create a nuisance for the restaurant.'

'It's not the Kruger Park, Richard. They're not baboons. A little charity won't go amiss.'

'I realise that, but just remember that charity is sometimes another word for expediency.'

'Oh for god's sake, this isn't an opinion column. They're young boys.' Catherine drunkenly rummaged through her purse.

Shaunelle resolved their frustrated standoff. She had slipped through the front door and shooed the two boys away with an irritated gesture of her hand. Standing outside, she waved. Catherine waved back.

'Do you ever think how things would have been different if we had kept it?' Richard continued to stare out of the window.

'You mean her,' Catherine corrected him.

'What do you mean, her?'

'It was a girl.' She grimaced, reached for her wine.

'You never told me.'

'You never asked.'

Hadn't he? It had all been such a rush before he left for Hubei province in China, a sudden change in photographer requiring a new letter of passage from the Chinese Embassy. And then his editor requested a rebriefing; the *New York Times* had trumped them on their angle on the story. Pressured by these things, he had treated the announcement of her pregnancy – revealed on a platform at Darlington station – like any other item on his pre-China checklist. Passport. Traveller's cheques. Rewritable disks. Draw money, pay for abortion. He had been that coldly methodical about it, leaving a sum of money and a blank cheque on their dresser. When he arrived back from China the envelope had still been there. Asked how it went, she flatly refused to speak about it, simply telling him that the stain had been removed.

'Do you still think about it a lot?'

'Not it, her.'

'You know what I mean.'

'Occasionally, I suppose.' There was a deadness about her voice as she said this. She refilled her glass, drank pensively.

'It was like Africa down there, you know,' she said, speaking into her glass.

'What are you talking about?'

'Tooting.'

'What about Tooting? I have no idea what you're on about.'

'It's where they did the procedure.'

'What the hell were you doing in south London?'

'I don't know, somehow I just ended up down there. I think it was a friend at work who recommended the hospital, I can't remember anymore. Or maybe I just wanted to see where the Northern Line would take me if I went south.'

'Jesus, Catherine, you never told me this.'

'You never asked.'

'Of course I did.'

'Maybe not hard enough.'

'So you had the abortion in Tooting?' He ran his hands through his tumble of hair, scratched angrily at his stubble.

'You know, I'm not lying, Richard, when I'm saying that it was like Africa. It really was just like one of those third-world hospitals you see on television. I was one of the only white faces. I still remember this big woman who sat next to me. She had a flower-patterned dress on. We eventually ended up chatting. No, scrap that, she counselled. I think I was crying.'

'I can't believe you never told me any of this.'

'You never asked, Rich. You were too busy with your god-forsaken dams in China.'

He dropped his head, tried to remember where Tooting was on the Northern Line. Sorry seemed like such a flimsy word. Shaunelle slipped the bill between them with a cautious smile.

It was noisy outside the restaurant when they exited it. The cool Atlantic air was filled with the sound of thudding bass from the cars parked outside the disco. The cars were parked two, some of them three deep, cheap cars with chromed rims. He put his arm around Catherine after she drunkenly stumbled. Sorry was such a flimsy word, he repeated. She fell asleep almost immediately after she lay down.

The hotel's bare garden was almost visible now from his position on the balcony. Morning was here. What would they have named her? It was a new, slightly haunting thought: her, not it. What would she have looked like? The women in his family had always been slightly overweight. He suddenly found himself thinking about his mother, his female cousins, Alison, Saltburn. He tried to imagine the salt sting between Catherine's legs as their child, only notionally now, was sucked from her womb.

He shut the hotel door gently so as not to wake her. Maybe a stroll along the beach would clear his head. He stumbled down the stairs drunkenly, mumbled something at the lone security guard as he ventured into the early morning quiet. Walking across the beach to the water's edge, Richard regretted not wearing a jacket. Midsummer or not, it was cold. How right his father had been.

'What do you want to take her up there for? It's *kak* there, only good for fishing and being alone.'

Tired, his mind exhausted, he sat himself down on the beach. He trawled his fingers through the soft sand, gathering all the flotsam that stuck between them, neatly stacking the debris in front of him. After a while he stopped. The sun was breaking through the mist. He looked down at the mound of junk he had collected between his legs. Just cigarette stubs, bits of fishing net and dried kelp. Not even a gift of stones.

The magic of numbers

Winning, it struck Beryl Vincent, her white-gloved hands fastened to the steering wheel in a perfect ten-to-two pose, her eyes fixed on the undulations of the relentlessly straight road ahead – winning was just a sound. It was not, she thought, an emotion. It was just a dull, metallic din, the clamour of perfectly like coins pouring from beneath a slot machine, a predictable mechanical hum. It was a sound that had somehow come to fill the quiet emptiness of her life since Frank's death.

'Well, let's hope we have better luck today in Witbank,' she said, the spry ambition of her words belying a nagging fatigue she had felt incapable of shaking off in recent months. Beryl was sixty-eight.

Daniel was silent.

'Fool,' she mumbled. A sleek Mercedes zoomed past at high speed. Her white Toyota Corolla momentarily veered left across the yellow line into the emergency lane. Daniel flinched but said nothing. He looked resolutely at the road ahead, his hands neatly cupped in his lap.

The two had not exchanged a word since Beryl's hatchback had passed through the gradually tapering hills near Donkerhoek, on the far eastern outskirts of Pretoria. That was 80 kilometres ago. Not that these lapses unsettled her, she was used to the silences, the spare dialogue that passed as conversation between them. After so many luckless journeys to the townships of Gauteng, she had grown quite accustomed to Daniel's reserve, the way he proffered subtle gestures instead of speech. To the unobservant outsider it would have appeared like an unforgivably mute exchange, but not for Beryl. Despite his taciturn manner, she recorded their conversations in the way he declined his slowly greying head of hair, or gently pursed his lips to form the vague outline of a smile. Things were never truly silent when he was around.

A thin man in his late fifties, Daniel was Beryl's garden help. For the past five years he had lived in the small creosote-coloured hut behind Beryl's garage. Before that, when she still lived in Brooklyn, he had occupied an unpainted room adjoining the hothouse. It was the house where Frank had quietly passed away, his slippers neatly tucked beneath the bed.

'If we don't win today, this'll be the last time,' Beryl ventured as a sign flashed by. Witbank 20 km.

'Maybe we will be lucky today, Madam.'

'Maybe,' Beryl replied.

He had a grey smell about him. Stale cigarette smoke. She loathed the musty odour. It reminded her of Frank, of the lung cancer that had stolen him away. Looking from her rear-view mirror, Beryl slipped a sideways glance at Daniel. What was he watching? The road ahead offered little more than a blank monotony.

Even before they reached the outskirts of Witbank, the town made its presence felt. An acrid smell filtered into the car, its source a series of smokestacks that towered over the misshapen black wattles on her right. The sign indicated ten kilometres.

What was the point of all of this? The thought came unexpectedly, like the smell. Surely there was no point to all of this stupidity? Why was she wasting her Saturday afternoons like this? Beryl tried to counter the doubts by concentrating on another, singular thought: winning. It was a sound, she reminded herself, winning was definitely a sound. It was also a township. Winning was the jubilant eruption of sound heard only in a township. It had been Mrs Landsman who had first shared this little known fact with her.

'It's obscene,' Mrs Landsman had declared. 'R30 million!'

Beryl knew precisely what her friend was referring to. She had also read the newspaper article about an elderly black artisan from Johannesburg. The man had won the lottery, his life irrevocably changed when a series of six numbers delivered a seismic windfall. Beryl quietly sipped her tea from a porcelain cup.

An acquaintance from the days when Beryl had owned a dry-cleaning business in a small shopping centre in Brooklyn, Mrs Landsman had in recent years become a close friend. A defiantly blonde mother of two, and grandmother of three and widow, she also shared a curious interest in the magic of numbers. On more than one occasion she had accompanied Beryl to some or other far-flung casino. Places like Meropa Casino in Polokwane, and Swaziland's Ezulwini Sun, the latter a three-day adventure marred by a blowout on a forested road between Ermelo and Oshoek, on the Swaziland border.

'I'm convinced it's just a waste of money,' Beryl had stated, delicately replacing her cup in its saucer.

'Not if you're black,' retorted Mrs Landsman.

'What do you mean?'

'Well, I heard that you have a better chance of winning the lottery if you buy your ticket in a township.' Mrs Landsman spoke the words with a privileged tone.

'Remember Dorothy? Her son is an accountant with SARS now. He told her that they *engineer* the wins to benefit people from poor areas.'

'Do you mean to say that if I buy a ticket in Mamelodi I have a better chance of winning than getting one from Carlos up the road?' Beryl asked.

'That's what the young man seems to think.'

'Really,' Beryl responded, more curiously than disbelievingly.

'Yes, but you won't catch me buying a lottery ticket in Mamelodi, even if the jackpot is R30 million.'

'Yes, quite.'

Beryl had initially shrugged off Mrs Landsman's declaration. Too improbable, she had reasoned, lying in bed alone. 'It's just another racist conspiracy theory,' her son had also laughed over the phone from Southampton. Despite this, she nonetheless found herself constantly coming back to Mrs Landsman's assertion. Surely it was impossible to engineer chance to benefit some and exclude others, she had reasoned. Although with computers …

As the weeks passed, the narrative also seemed to become ever stickier, ever more probable each time she saw a newspaper headline.

The first one appeared a few weeks after her tea engagement with Mrs Landsman. BLACK PENSIONER WINS R15 MILLION. The bold simplicity of the statement rattled her. A month or so later she spotted another. HOMELESS PERSON WINS LOTTERY. Something ridiculous swiftly seemed almost plausible. As she lay down to sleep that night, a fantastical idea unexpectedly cohered in her mind. After breakfast the next morning, Beryl confronted her garden help.

'Do you play the lottery, Daniel?'

Daniel was busy preparing a bed of soil near her bedroom window in anticipation of spring.

'Sometimes,' he answered. He went on turning over the soil with a little spade.

'Where do you buy your tickets?'

Daniel dug the spade into a patch of earth, turned and looked up quizzically.

'At the café.'

'You mean from Carlos?'

'Mostly.'

'Do you ever play the lottery when you go home?'

'To the Winterveld, you mean, Madam?'

'Yes.'

'Sometimes, but that lottery, it is just a waste of money.' He turned and resumed his work.

Beryl looked at the man's grizzled hands. In spring they would remove a flowering petunia from its plastic seedling punnet and carefully place it in a small hole in the earth. Rain would do the rest.

'Is that all, Madam?' Daniel asked. He straightened himself upright, looking down at her.

'Um, not really,' Beryl responded.

It had been almost four months since Beryl first presented her awkward proposal to Daniel. Every Saturday, Daniel was to accompany her to a remote petrol station or corner café – preferably in a township, or at least adjacent. She called it a freelance security job. In exchange for accompanying her on these hopeful ramblings, she promised him a twenty per cent stake in whatever winnings she made. An empowerment deal, she joked with her conscience.

'Here?' Beryl asked as they approached a cluttered settlement. The signboard read: Kromdraai/Clewer 1 km.

'I'm not sure.'

'No, it can't be,' Beryl said, looking at the government housing project that had recently been erected in a plot of veld. But for a few tentative extensions and additions made to some of the homesteads, they all looked the same, were geometric duplicates of one another. A vague thought nested itself in her mind: democracy was not the cheerful collision of colours on the national flag, it was this – the even-hued monotone of these homesteads. The car swooped past the Kromdraai/Clewer off-ramp. They would take the next off-ramp. The car passed over the Brug River.

'Unless we get lucky today, this will definitely be the last time we do this,' Beryl repeated. 'There's nothing out at these places.' Daniel nodded his head, was silent.

These places. The words prompted a quick tabulation of all the new and unfamiliar places she had visited over the past few months: Mamelodi, Ga-Rankuwa, Soshanguve, Eersterus and Atteridgeville. Although familiar by name, most of them had been alien as an actuality. After seeing them all she didn't think much of these sprawling communes, these denials dragged from the past into the present. But even their curious strangeness passed. As her day trips involved ever more distant and unfamiliar locations, so the anticipation and vigour with which she had initially approached the enterprise was slowly eclipsed, replaced by routine and disappointment. Not even Tweefontein, in Bronkhorstspruit, where Happy Sindane lived, had offered anything. Hope was now simply a predictable thing, the act of travelling somewhere new only to discover that it looked like somewhere else. Poor. Dusty. Congested. Maybe Witbank would be different.

The sign indicated Schoongezicht/KwaGuqa/Ferrobank one kilometre, and was followed immediately by another sign. HI-JACKING HOTSPOT. The triangular red sign featured a prominent exclamation mark. They used the same mark to warn about pedestrians and potholes.

A taxi abruptly pushed in front of her. She braked hard. Daniel reached for the handrail.

'Damn fool!' Beryl shouted out.

She followed the metallic blue kombi down the off-ramp. *If you would like to know about life after death, ask the taxi driver*, read a vinyl-cut sticker on the rear window. Above it was a pair of hands held in prayer. Something about the image grabbed her. They slowed to a crawl. The taxi turned right towards Schoongezicht and KwaGuqa. Mindful of the earlier exclamation mark, Beryl slipped past the stop sign, turned left.

The car pulled onto a dusty margin a short distance from the T-junction, next to a dry and winter-black vlei. A veld fire had recently destroyed much of it, leaving only fire-ruined stalks poking from the ground. She hated winter landscapes, so brutal, so full of litter, so evidently inhabited. A confusion of shacks looked over the vlei, and was framed by geometric mounds of soil, quite similar to the ones she had seen in Boksburg, where Frank had been born. The only difference was their colour. These ones were black, like the colour of the small stain on Frank's lung that had eventually taken him away.

'I thought we could go double or nothing today.' Beryl placed a pair of reading glasses on the edge of her nose and peered into the handbag placed on her lap.

Daniel said nothing. He knew the ritual. She passed him the envelope.

A R20 note bought you eight chances, delineated from A to H, six numbers listed lengthways in each row.

'And here, take this one too.' Beryl held out another envelope. 'It's something extra, for helping out over the past few months. I know you would rather be watching soccer. It's not much but maybe you can put it towards your daughter's schooling or something.'

Daniel took the envelope. He lifted the unsealed flap and

curiously peered inside. It contained two blue bank notes.

'Thank you, Madam.'

'Don't spend it on the lottery, hey. You've seen what a waste it is.'

Daniel smiled. He had a single front tooth. 'Maybe it is not a waste,' he offered. 'It is important to believe in something, Madam.'

'You could be right.'

Looking out of her window at the desolate winter landscape, an unresolved thought from earlier came to her again. She inhaled deeply. What is the purpose of this? Near the marshes, industrial piping jutted aimlessly from the ground, the exposed length serving as a makeshift footbridge connecting two adjacent communities of shacks. What does it mean to win, to hold something more than the disappointment of a fistful of coins in a paper cup?

Watching a young woman negotiating the makeshift footbridge, she allowed the answer she had been avoiding to declare itself finally: buying a lottery ticket in a township was no guarantee of winning. Nothing did not automatically beget something. Mrs Landsman was wrong.

'How many rooms does your house have?' Beryl asked as she steered her car back onto the tarmac.

'Three.'

'And does it have a garden?'

'Yes, but not such a good one. The dogs are always digging things up.'

'Stray dogs?'

'Pardon?'

'Um, other people's dogs, runaways, um, wild dogs.'

'Ah no,' Daniel laughed. 'My dogs.'

'You have pets?'

'Yes, two dogs.' He flashed another embarrassed smile.

'Two, good heavens, I didn't know that. What are their names?'

'Sheba and Dickie.'

'Dickie! You mean like the Dickie I had when you first came to work for me?'

'Yes, Madam,' Daniel replied, his hand muffling a shy giggle. 'He looked like your Dickie when my daughter brought him home so I decided to call him by the same name.'

The telltale sign came into view abruptly and Beryl quickly slowed down, steering her car into the crowded lot of the BP. Finding a lottery vendor in a township was always easy: you just had to look for a long queue snaking from a garage or spaza. She dropped Daniel close to the line and looked for a spot to park. By now the curious stares and occasional derisive comment meant nothing to her. It was just a routine: park, wait, leave. Lose.

Today, though, she fixed her eyes on Daniel, watched as the line slowly drew him closer to the front. He was still wearing his blue overall and earnestly looked ahead, his stare rarely wavering as the line shuffled and snaked. Dickie. The cheeky Jack Russell had been a gift from Frank. In the end, the little terror had outlived him by two years, the ignominy of the dog's worn-out joints and ground-down teeth recently ended by a veterinarian's needle. To think that the dog had somehow found a second life out in the Winterveld, in that barren wilderness flanking the road to the Carousel casino.

The movement of the line finally swallowed Daniel into the interior of the garage shop. She would have to tell her son about it – then again, possibly not. It was too quaintly disconcerting and unsettling, the sudden calm that was unexpectedly derived from Daniel's revelation. Beryl snorted out loud. To think that peace of mind could be had here in a township in the middle of nowhere. Her mind was running away with things.

She turned up the radio to drown out the discord of her thoughts. The Blue Bulls had lost, again. Officials in a rural Indian province were cajoling tax evaders into paying by employing drummers to beat instruments outside their homes. It would be cloudless but cold tomorrow. Suddenly, it came to her. Maybe the magic of numbers did exist, just not in Pretoria. Quite possibly the prize was closer to Johannesburg. It was not an unreasonable proposition. Maybe all they needed to do was change direction, head further south. As Daniel came loping towards the car, Beryl resolved that she would speak to him on Monday. Tomorrow was his day off.

A chance meeting

I found the dictionary in the veld, a rain-scarred book of words laid open and stiff on a koppie in South Hills. It was partially obscured by tufts of late summer grass and lay open on page 110, taut and unbending in the breeze, just like a corpse. I still remember the page number, partly because of the strangeness of the first two words that greeted me as I stooped to pick it up. *Benzol.* I had never come across the word before, nor the second, *benzoline.* I suppose it was the peculiarity of this detail that distracted my attention from the silver water-tower hovering over the veld. It was the not knowing what those words meant.

The dictionary's sun-dried pages were home to a small colony of ants. They looked like little black commas as they scurried to and fro across the open page, agitated punctuation marks that revealed an interest in exploring my arm. I shook off the dictionary and closed it. It was a 1959 copy of the *Concise Oxford Dictionary of Current English*, the fourth edition, its cloth cover still faintly blue. I turned it over to look at the alphabetical list on page 110 again. *Bequeath.* It was the third word and means something about leaving, or to quote the posh old dictionary, to transmit to posterity, which I presume was the effect of leaving the dictionary in a veld overlooking City Deep and Johannesburg's buff-coloured mine dumps.

It took some effort to force the dictionary to close, less of a struggle to pry the cover from its flyleaf. It was then that the book's owner announced himself: Sylvesta. His name was neatly printed in angular blue letters on the inside of the dictionary's hardbound cover, the thick ink line suggesting a very deliberate gesture, proud too. A sequence of two numbers followed, one on top of the other. The first was a seven-digit number (Johannesburg maybe?), below it a cell number.

The last telephone number impressed an obvious fact on me: the dictionary hadn't been lying in the veld since 1959; Cell C had only started operating in 2002. And then there was that name, Sylvesta. Not Sylvester, as in Stallone, just Sylvesta. Neither Silvester, which I later discovered was the name of two popes, a name with Roman origins, from the Latin word *silva*, meaning 'of the forest'; just Sylvesta.

Not that the particularity of these details held my attention for long. I hadn't come to South Hills to learn new words; I was here for the silver water tower. I tossed the old dictionary back on the ground and returned to my camera, which was propped on a tripod and aimed at the tower. Of course, I don't admit to the idea of photographing water towers being particularly original, even though the bulbous hunk of round metal resting on a thin pipette-like stem was certainly unique, by local standards at least. Most of the towers dotted across Johannesburg's semi-arid landscapes are concrete, not metal, like the graffiti-coloured one on Northcliff Hill, which is a rather common example of the form.

The idea of photographing the city's water towers came to me one Saturday morning in the basement of Collectors' Treasury, on Commissioner Street. While sniffling and sneezing my way through the store's overcrowded rows of books, I found a copy of Bernd and Hilla Becher's *Wassertürme* ('R850/US$115 – 1st Edition, Scarce,' stated the writing pencilled onto the flyleaf). Something about the banality of the German couple's decade-long project intrigued me, the meditative glance it offered of obscure European and American industrial architecture. Paging through the book in the basement, my nose dribbling, I had an idea; like an apprentice I would copy their style, the only difference being that my focus would be limited to the 33 water towers scattered across Johannesburg.

Standing next to my camera I took another light reading. I had arrived too early and the sun was still far too bright for a photograph. Hands cupped over my eyes, I looked at the arc it still had to travel before it would meet with the horizon line. There was nothing I could do but perfect the composition. I looked into the viewfinder again, focusing my lens on the upside-down water tower held fixed in the dark beneath the cloth draped over my head. The upside-down tower looked almost like the one the Bechers had photographed in Brookville, Pennsylvania, in 1974, a futuristic industrial object set amidst a pastoral landscape. Uncanny.

Absolutely certain that my composition was now perfect, I returned to trampling bored, roving arcs around my camera. I saw the dictionary again, still open on page 110, then an empty beer bottle, its label long washed from its surface, an old tyre, its tread worn smooth, a briefcase.

I bent down to look at the piece of luggage. It didn't strike me as being an expensive briefcase, just a pretend thing, something to look self-important with in the big city. The briefcase had been brutalised, its innards torn out like those of a gutted animal. Amongst the scattered mess: a series of English exercise sheets; officious-looking documents (bleached of all personalised inscriptions); a pen (a yellow Bic); a photograph of a car (a red Cressida); lining (from the briefcase); a used-up cellphone voucher (Cell C, R30). It was simply a tedious mess, no blood, just useless junk.

Maybe its owner had been mugged, I reasoned. Who the hell walks along a path cutting through the bush from South Rand Road towards Regents Park and Roseacre with a briefcase? Or a camera, for that matter? I looked over my shoulder. Sylvesta? Intrigued at the possibility this bit of knowledge suggested, I paced back to the dictionary, counting the steps. Ten. Suddenly I found myself trying to visualise the crime: a knife (probably a metal blade with a duct-tape handle) held against the tremor of Sylvesta's throat. I tried to imagine his characterless terror as his assailants issued their blunt demand, for his wallet, his cellphone, his briefcase, his dictionary. And then their reaction when they discovered he was a foreigner, a man who spoke in faltering English, who begged for clemency in a strange tongue.

Then again, maybe they (a group of youths, no doubt) had simply stolen the briefcase from Sylvesta's home, while he was out at the corner café buying cigarettes or a pay-as-you-go voucher for his cellphone. The possibilities were limitless.

Returning to my camera I found myself increasingly uninterested by the water tower, which, after all, was my reason for journeying to this obscure piece of veld in the first place. The name written on the flyleaf of the dictionary, the briefcase lying spilt open in the veld behind me; I was all of a sudden involved. What did this Sylvesta look like? Doubtless he was black, a recent immigrant, possibly from Mozambique or Angola, which would account for the Latinised name. He wasn't a man of Portuguese extraction resident in Kenilworth or La Rochelle, I decided. Somehow my mind was determined to believe in the first possibility, that he looked just like one of those men shown in profile on barbershop signs, the ones they sold in curio stores in Rosebank.

Of course, I could simply telephone him to verify my freewheeling logic. I had my cellphone with me. It crossed my mind more than a few times as I circled my camera, listlessly kicking at rubbish and sand clods in the veld. Something in me resisted the urge; possibly it was the oddness of how it would all come out.

'Hullo.'

'Um, yes, hello … My name is Andy … Um, I …'

'Hullo, who's dis?' (Sylvesta no doubt has a deep, sonorous voice, a richly flavoured accent.)

'Hello, yes sorry … Andy, my name is Andy Hughes. I found your dictionary, I mean your briefcase lying in the veld … just off South Rand Road … in Moffat Park.'

'Who dis? How you get dis number?'

'I'm sorry … is that Sylvesta?'

'Maybe.'

Oh hell, you know how it is, you can't just phone a stranger and tell him you found his missing briefcase in the veld while on a ramble taking photographs of water towers. Still, I did think about calling his number.

Looking west again, I saw that the sun was intent on lingering in the late Saturday afternoon sky. I checked my light meter again. Still a short wait more. Much to my irritation, I saw that an elderly security guard had appeared inside the water tower's fenced-off grounds. He was seated on a red plastic chair (a Coke crate actually), positioned directly in front of the silver structure I was aiming to photograph. I would have to ask him to move.

Walking through the straw-coloured grass I found myself again contemplating the evidence, thinking about what it suggested about the little drama that had unfolded in the veld. Looked at objectively, it appeared as if the briefcase had been stolen elsewhere, possibly a taxi. There was a makeshift taxi stop situated across the road from the veld, right next to the water tower. Maybe the guard had seen something from behind his concrete slatted barricade, or heard a muffle of voices late one night. Walking past a burnt heap of magazines, I pondered the odd relationship of the dictionary to the briefcase, the distance travelled by the one from the other.

Maybe they were unrelated, it dawned on me. Couldn't be, I countered. Too much to suggest that the dictionary belonged to the gutted briefcase. Possibly the robbers had briefly considered keeping it, then chucked it, leaving the 1549-page book (enclosed by a hardbound cover) a short distance from the briefcase. Beset (the last word on page 110) by this thought, I greeted the elderly man.

'Hello.'

He had an insubstantial grey beard and wore brown army surplus boots that seemed mismatched with the black uniform. He simply nodded his head.

'I'm taking a photograph of the water tower. I was hoping you might be able to move out of the picture for a second.'

'Why do you want to photograph this building?' he queried from his seat, his tone unexpectedly authoritative.

'Sorry, my name is Andy,' I offered apologetically. 'I am a photographer. I am taking photos of all the water towers in Johannesburg, for a private project. I came here specially to take a photo of this one ... from Bryanston.'

I hoped the lie would impress him; I lived in Braamfontein.

'No photos here.'

'But I haven't had any problems before, even this morning when I went to Dobsonville.'

Another lie. While I did drive past the concrete water towers in Dobsonville this morning, five times, I was too afraid to stop. The eerily domestic landscape in the vicinity of the tower confounded my expectations of Soweto.

'No photos,' he repeated.

The man's abrupt conversational manner suggested that he wouldn't be drawn out on the subject. I thanked him and returned to my camera. A quick glance at my light meter showed the sun to be just right. I quickly took my shot. It would be the first to include a human presence, useful perhaps for indicating scale, I reasoned. I packed up. The security guard was still seated on his portable throne, purposefully watching my every move as I walked towards my Golf. I waved again as I drove past, a taunt. I had furtively tucked the dictionary into my camera bag.

The old man's rebuff wasn't the first time I had encountered frustrations with my photography. Before my current preoccupation with water towers I had worked on another project, something I had hoped would gain me shelf space on a display rack at Exclusive Books. Quite which shelf I remain uncertain of, travel guides possibly. My idea: a series of guidebooks documenting interesting walks in and around Johannesburg. Historical walks, architectural rambles, naturalist hikes, artistic saunters, environmental marches. Each illustrated with my photographs, of course.

Working two jobs, one as a part-time lecturer at a private photography school, the other as a photographic printer at a professional laboratory near Sandton City, I get to see a lot of what is being photographed in Johannesburg. Mostly it is package shots of cosmetics and cereal boxes, or fashion photographs from the Maldives, the interiors of smart private homes, postcard views of Johannesburg from Yeoville ridge, nervous views out of inner-city flat blocks and, particularly of late, sweetly sentimental photographs of shanty settlements. I rarely encounter anything that shows the denuded texture of Johannesburg, its crumbling Art Deco architecture and half-excavated mine dumps, nothing at all on its forgotten rivers and strip mall architecture. There is a strange will towards amnesia in the commercial dealings and imaginings of Johannesburg.

Experience, however, soon proved me to be an arrogant apprentice. There was already a definitive book on old Johannesburg's architecture, historical walks aplenty, even the odd, precocious artistic saunter. As for the rivers, no one cared about them. Of Johannesburg's two major watercourses, the Jukskei and Klip rivers, the former was a mess of fenced-off public space and plastic bottles curdled along its banks, the latter an apocalyptic no-man's-land near its source, at New Canada and Riverlea. For six months I took no pictures, my adopted city, Johannesburg, an elusive subject. Then I came across *Wassertürme*. I would be a copyist, I resolved. Through this basest form of flattery I would relook at the city anew, and possibly even learn something about myself.

Once home, I put the dictionary in a Pick 'n Pay packet and stored it beneath the sink, next to the insect repellent. It didn't stay there long. After watching a roundup of the day's sport, I fetched the book and placed it on my coffee table, on top of the unread *Saturday Star*. It was a bestial (from page 111) object, a dirty mass rather than a book of discrete pages conjoined by a binding. More pliant now after my initial encounter with it, the book closed quite easily. I opened it to its flyleaf and dialled the cellphone number. A standardised prerecorded voice, best described as droll, repeated the number 0-8-4-6-6-1-3-1-1-3 and then summarily stated that it did not exist. I tried the number again. The female voice repeated what she had told me earlier. The number didn't exist despite the angular blue statement of fact written into the dictionary.

I tried the land-line number.

'Nest Inn.' The speed with which the voice answered the phone startled me.

'Um, can I please speak to Sylvesta, please?'

'Who?' Her manner was casual.

'Sylvesta!'

'He's not here.' Indifferent too.

'Is there any way I could get in touch with him? I have something of his and I can't seem to get hold of him on his cellphone.'

'What do you want to give to him?'

'A book.'

'A book?'

'A dictionary.'

She paused briefly on this. I heard chewing gum sounds crackle through the receiver.

'He's not here.'

'You said so,' I tartly reminded her.

Silence.

'Hello?'

'He's not here but his wife is here, do you want to speak to her?'

I was mildly stunned. I had never bargained on this, on my lonely Park Station immigrant enjoying the comfort of a wife.

'Hello? Do you want to speak to her?'

'No, no, that's okay. Let me take down the address, I'll drop off the book sometime tomorrow.'

I slept fitfully.

Looking at myself in the rear-view mirror before setting out to return the dictionary to its owner, I saw that I had burnt in the sun yesterday. My forehead was sweetly pink. I drove around the block twice, the dictionary now wrapped up in a Woolworth's packet and resting on the passenger seat. The residential hotel was on Smit Street, very close to Park Station, close to the old Hillbrow Hospital too, a short walk from the Constitutional Court. The display board read Nest In, which I suppose is correct in a sense, the preposition implying much the same meaning as the noun, a welcoming call to enter. It took me a while to do that. On my third loop past the Civic and rundown YMCA, I saw a car pull out from a parking space near the hotel. I parked.

For some time I just sat there, pretending in an off-hand manner to be waiting while reading the *Sunday Times*. It was mid-morning. Judging by the get-up worn by most of the passers-by, a religious spirit had descended over Hillbrow. Christian Zionist men in khaki uniforms and conductor caps flanked women dressed in blue and white robes. A man in a dark suit who had just left the hotel opened the passenger door of a dilapidated white Mazda. A woman primly dressed in a multicoloured dress, her hair a profusion of neat curls, stepped into the car. After the ten o'clock news on SAfm, I stepped out of my car and entered the hotel.

The reception area was neatly kept, and in truth little more than an elevator lobby. The former residential block had never been designed to function as a hotel. I approached the young man seated behind a desk that had been placed in an alcove in the corner.

'Hello. Is Sylvesta here? I have a book that belongs to him.'
The young man smiled.

'Yes, Mr Shiabe.'

'No, Sylvesta,' I corrected him.

'Yes, that's Mr Shiabe. Let me call up and see if he's in.'

'No, no, that's okay,' I protested as he turned to press a button on the intercom behind him. I wasn't prepared for this, any of this.

'Just give him the book, tell him I found it in …'

'Hello, Mr Shiabe, there is a man here to see you.'

'No, look it's fine,' I said placing the book on the counter, back-pedalling. 'Just tell him I found it on a koppie in South Hills.'

I ran. I don't know why I did, or what the young man in the reception made of my lurching move to get away as he spoke with Sylvesta. I couldn't stay; I couldn't face the awkward moment as Sylvesta exited the lift, his slight moustache and frowning grin offset by his black-framed reading glasses. All the neatly constructed fictions in my head would have been detonated by the moment his hand, warm and fleshy, grasped mine. The possibility of these very particular and physical details scared me, just like the specifics of how he negotiated his new life without his dictionary. Instead of waiting for the answer to all the innumerable questions in my head, I ran, to my car, to the familiarity of street names, suburbs, buildings, rivers, objects. People scared me.

Not that my encounter with Sylvesta was entirely without reward. While seated in the car waiting to enter the hotel, I had been intrigued by the bold modernist typeface announcing the building across the road, Waverly Mansions (248 Smit Street). Unlike the hand-painted signage for Nest In, Waverly Mansions declared its existence with a lean Univers font. It was beautiful in its simplicity, unencumbered by serifs, totally distinct in form from the Art Nouveau typeface that proclaimed Ursula Mansions, on Klein Street. Speeding away from my near encounter with the owner of the battered dictionary, I suddenly had an idea for another project.

The road to Rephile

'Hey, Papa Crocs, how long have you been driving trucks?'

'It's been twenty-seven years now.'

'Ha, about the time Mandela was in jail.'

The greying man seated opposite Moses Skweyiya in the bar smiled, wanly. The truth of the comparison stung. Twenty-seven years.

'I suppose, I've never thought about it that way,' he said, speaking in a slow, determined voice. 'Just like Mandela.'

Sam 'Papa Crocs' Ngwenya drained the last of the beer into a clear plastic cup.

'Let's drink to Mandela.' Moses raised his cup. 'To Mandela!"

'To Mandela.' The beer was warm and flat, tasted awful. Sam excused himself for the toilet. His bladder wasn't good with beer; he would probably be up and down the whole night because of it.

He threaded his way past four youths standing around a battered pool table. Despite their buckling legs and drunken shouting they were alert and looked at Sam with measured hostility. He made sure not to bump anyone. Papa Crocs, he hadn't heard the nickname in years. It was only Moses who called him by the stupid name. What was it, twelve years now since Germiston Transport went under?

Sam slipped past the curtain into the toilet. Moses, he thought, peeing, he hadn't expected to bump into him. He was a youth fresh off the farm via Park Station when he first arrived at the company, all wide-eyed and full of jokes. For two years he had been his loader, the stupid nickname invented on one of the lonely routes they had driven together. Papa Crocs, it was harmless enough, Ngwenya meaning 'crocodile', just a bit of respectful tomfoolery really. He had always liked the boy.

While washing his hands he looked around the toilet. It was clean enough but like the restaurant it was bare, not what he remembered. He made his way back past the young pool players, saw two girls, not many years older than his daughter, sitting near the bar, their attention fixed on the television propped above it. Things had definitely changed since his last visit five years ago. He still remembered the old Wimpy franchise. All that this Yebo Yes Tavern offered by way of a menu was a messy scribble of words written on the rear of a beer carton. The new toll road must have been bad for Mr Frank.

Driving down the alternative route earlier this afternoon, Sam had looked forward to seeing Mr Frank, the cantankerous proprietor of Frölich Motors. He had always enjoyed the big man's nostalgic recollections of life in Stuttgart and Windhoek, his larger-than-life story of his arrival in South Africa, on the back of a freight train, loaded with little more than a rucksack and youthful ambition. When Rephile was still young, a mouth of milk teeth, he had often told her about 'the strange German man from the north'. He was just one of an ensemble of fantastic characters from the road that he would use to lull his only daughter to sleep. How things had changed. Rephile didn't need bed stories anymore; the TV seemed to tell her all the stories she wanted to know nowadays.

'How's your wife?' Moses asked as Sam seated himself down.

'Fine,'

'And your daughter … what's her name?'

'Rephile, she's fine too. She's twelve now.'

'Twelve! I didn't realise it's been so long since the company closed.'

'May 1993.'

'Eish, you have a good memory, Papa Crocs. Some things never change.'

'What about you, are you married?'

'Me, never. I don't need to get married.'

'Why?'

'I want to live my own life. Anyway, I have a woman in every town. I don't need a wife, not now.'

'How old are you now, Moses?'

'I'll be thirty next October.'

'You will need a wife soon, then.'

'Maybe, but not now. For now I'm not restricted, I'm unlimited.'

Sam thought about the meaning of his acquaintance's odd choice of words, the determined sense of confidence with which he spoke them. Unrestricted. Unlimited. He had never spoken like that when he was young. He married Zandi when he was twenty-two, started driving trucks three years after.

'I'm getting another, do you want one?' Moses said, sweeping the two empty beer bottles from the table.

Sam nodded his head in agreement and then immediately regretted it as Moses walked off. The low, insistent thud of the kwaito music had given him a headache. He rarely drank beer, just on special occasions, if his chance encounter with an old contact could be described as that. He should go sleep, he thought, looking at the television where the young women were seated. They were nodding their heads in sync with the beat. I'm old, I don't belong here. This music is strange. He immediately checked himself: Rephile likes this music too.

Moses returned with two cold beers.

'Which company are you working for now, Papa Crocs?'

'It's a small one in Roodepoort. The pay is not so good but it is nearer Soweto. You know my wife has asked me to make a plan. She says I must get a job where I can knock off in the evenings, and come back home. This was the best I could find.'

'And you? How is your company?' He looked at his companion's faded overall. Even with the company patch removed from the pocket, he immediately recognised it. Moses must have taken it with him when he received his retrenchment package.

'Eish, times are tough now. I think it's better that I pack up this job, Papa Crocs, just drink. I don't make any money doing this job. Like now, for example, I'm on a one-way trip to Durban. It's just a piece job. They gave me train fare to come back, third class. It's better if I find my own transport back.'

'I'm sorry, I'm only going to Newcastle. If I was going to Durban you could come back with me.'

'Thanks, Papa Crocs, you are a good man … just like Mandela.' A cheeky smile came across his face. He toasted Sam, repeated the comparison loud enough for the group of youths to stop their game and look up. Sam gulped down a mouthful of beer. The game resumed. Moses stood up.

'I'm going to talk to my new wife over there,' he said, nodding his head in the direction of the bar.

Sam watched his former loader stroll across the room. His stride was confident; he knew what he wanted. He stopped next to a woman standing alone at the counter. She was wearing an Orlando Pirates T-shirt that was way too big for her. It looked like a dress. Maybe that was the fashion these days? Sam did not recall seeing her earlier when he walked from the toilet. She didn't seem part of the noisy pageant grouped around the pool table. She must have slipped in while they were talking. Maybe this was his cue to exit. He would leave the rest of his beer for Moses; he had a healthy enough appetite for the stuff. He motioned to get up.

'It's still early, Papa Crocs, where are you going?' Moses had his arm hitched over the shoulder of the woman. He pulled up another chair.

'Meet Neo.' Her smile seemed more like a scowl.

What kind of name is that? It sounds like something off the TV, something that one of the gyrating presenters on SABC 1 late at night called themselves. Neo-Dineo? He pushed his beer over to Moses.

'What, no more, Papa Crocs?'

'No, I think I must go sleep soon. I must be in Newcastle early tomorrow morning.'

'Hey, you must be getting old …'

'… just like Mandela.' He managed to beat his compatriot to it this time.

She had hard, sunken eyes, Sam noticed, her scrawny face not totally unattractive. She wore a large scar above her left eye. A cruel night with a drunken man, he imagined.

'So what happened to that truck Mr Rooks promised you at Germiston?'

'The lawyers took that truck. They auctioned it off. You know, sometimes I still see that truck of mine, fleet number 2701. That was my truck. Somebody has a truck in his name that is actually mine. Even now, it makes my heart bitter.'

Moses was not really listening. His hand was playfully cupped around one of Neo's breasts.

'And you, what happened to you after the company closed, Moses?'

'I learnt to enjoy *kwasa kwasa.*'

'What?'

'*Kwasa kwasa!* Hey, you know nothing, Papa Crocs. It is music, from Zambia.'

'I see. So how did you end up working in Zambia?'

Moses laughed. 'No, no, I was with a company that did long haul – into Africa.'

'Africa.' The word had a warm, unfamiliar taste in Sam's mouth as he repeated it. It tasted like cinnamon and mango and chilli all mixed up. He had never been further than Polokwane with his truck.

'So why did things turn out bad for you?'

Neo squirmed and slapped at Moses' hand. He had just pinched her nipple.

'That long-haul company, they were just crooks. They asked me to sign one of those owner–driver contracts when I started. I was very excited. It was a chance to be unlimited for real. But *daai ding is vokol, net* rubbish.' He spat the words out. 'They cheated me, didn't even register that truck in my name. When I came back from a trip to Zimbabwe, they fired me. They said there were too many of us drivers, not enough work. That empowerment story, I'm telling you, it's just words.'

Moses drank another mouthful of beer, wiping the back of his hand across his mouth afterwards. He was smiling again. Something about the outburst lingered, though, reminding Sam of something he had been thinking of earlier in the day. It suddenly asserted itself.

'You know, this government say they want to empower us but who is monitoring it?' The words felt awkward as they came out. He pressed on.

'You know, Moses, I'm not political, I don't like politics whatsoever but, you see, in this transport job of ours, there are pilots: they are well remembered. And then there are train drivers: they are well remembered. There are also captains of ships: they are well remembered. But us truck drivers …' He lost his train of thought. It was the beer; it always made his thoughts fuzzy, less concentrated.

'*Ai*, this old man, he is too serious. Go buy some more beer.' It was Neo.

Sam looked at her with interest. She had not spoken at all, merely poured beer for Moses whenever his cup was empty. She met his gaze blankly. There was no hostility in it, just an immeasurable rift. He looked at Moses. His eyes were bloodshot, his fingers playfully concerned with teasing at the ripened nipple silhouetted against her football jersey. He had spoken his words into a void. Sam dropped his head miserably.

How had he lost his train of thought like that? It had been so clear in his mind this morning when he was driving. He had been listening to Tim Modise on 702. Tim was discussing empowerment. His studio guest was a BEE expert. Sometimes, especially when they referred to a certain act of parliament, the talk went over his head but Tim always seemed to steer it back into his reach, making the educated man clarify his comments. It was why he liked Tim, why he had followed the radio journalist from his slot on SAfm to the static-infested medium-wave channel.

Thinking about the radio reminded him of his bed in the back of the truck. It was time to go sleep. This place wasn't for him anymore.

'Tell Moses I say goodbye.'

He felt guilty for slipping away while Moses was in the toilet. But his former loader was now his own man, he would have to live by his own choices now, make good of his new inheritance. In any case, they were no longer a team, not anymore.

A riverine mist had settled over the truck stop. Sam struggled through the haze, searching for his truck. He felt disappointed. He had hoped to see Mr Frank, laugh at his inconsequential jokes. Instead, he got caught in a beery conversation with someone he hadn't thought of in years. Getting into the truck, he wondered momentarily about Neo. She was, however, simply a springboard to other, more pressing thoughts. How long would Rephile still be comfortable nestling under the protective wing of her ageing parents? He didn't want the thought answered.

Sam lay down on his bunk bed, looked up at the photos he had stuck above his head with Prestik. It was not much but it was something, he thought, studying the photograph of his grey-bricked house in Chiawelo. How many times had he looked at this photo of his house on the southwestern reaches of Soweto? Rephile stood in the foreground, smiling, and just over her shoulder the house's number: 2841. It was painted in white freehand next to the front door. He looked at another photo. It was Rephile on her first day of school; he had been in Durban that day. And Zandi, she had a lonely smile. Twenty-seven years of loneliness. Just like Mandela, he joked to himself.

Had he built a similar shrine to his loneliness? Don't all men in prison? He smiled at the thought as he reached for the *Sowetan* newspaper he had brought with him. Nights were not the same without Jon Qwelane. After the bosses at 702 pulled him off the air, Sam's evenings were not quite the same. He missed Qwelane's purposely slow and rambling dialogue, the lack of urgency in his voice as he nonchalantly put down annoying callers, especially those from Cape Town. What had happened to Qwelane? Was this de-empowerment?

He turned to the sports section, studied the photograph of

the Pirates player. Rephile said she liked this Vilakazi fellow. Rephile. Lately she seemed less and less interested in where he had been and what he had seen. She was becoming like Zandi, distant. Rephile, to think they had waited so long for her.

'Right, we're back. You're listening to the Tim Modise Network on talk radio 702. As you know, today we have a special guest in our studio, former president Nelson Mandela. This is a rare opportunity for you to talk with Madiba. Call us now; the lines are open. Are you ready for the next caller, Mr Mandela?'

'Yes, Tim, I'm ready. You know I've been ready since 1990.'

'Great. Okay, I see we have Sam Ngwenya on the line. Hello Sam, you're live on air. What is your question for Mr Mandela?'

'Yes … hello, Tim, this is Sam. How are you, Tim?'

'I'm fine, Sam, what is it you want to ask Mr Mandela?'

'Tata Mandela, this is Sam. I am very excited to be speaking with you.'

'Thank you, Sam.'

'Okay, Sam, so what's your question? Remember, we have lots of callers waiting so make it quick and simple, please.'

'Sorry, Tim. Tata Mandela, you know I am a truck driver. Sometimes, well often, I am on the road. Recently, I read your book, Long Walk to Freedom. In it you say, "A man is not a man until he has a house of his own." I agree. But, in fact, I want to ask you about when you were in jail. Did you ever think about your first house in Orlando West during those years?'

'Now you are asking me a question, Sam. I don't know if I can remember that far back.'

'Am I right in saying that that was when you were married to your first wife, Evelyn, Mr Mandela?'

'Yes, Tim. I was still married to Evelyn. I had already moved from that house before I was sent to Robben Island, I was living with Winnie. But you know, Sam, I still remember that house, the pictures of Roosevelt, Churchill and Gandhi on my wall ...'

Sam sat up, the newspaper falling from his chest. The cabin's light was still on. He didn't recall switching the radio on when he climbed in, he thought, looking at the console where the radio was installed. It was off. Had he been dreaming all that nonsense? His bladder was full.

Climbing from his truck he could barely make out the garage and restaurant in the near distance. It was quiet. Lonely too. He peed a few paces from his truck. Once back inside, he checked the radio again. It was definitely off. Wrapping a blanket around himself, he looked at the photographs again: the house, Zandi, Rephile. The darkness was absolute and silent when he switched the light off.

'Hello, Sam, are you there? Sam?'

'Yes, Tim, I'm here. Sorry, you know this medium-wave station of yours can be funny sometimes, especially if there is lightning. I think it must be storming somewhere; I couldn't hear you or Tata Mandela.'

'Well, you must be lucky today, Sam. My producer has just told me that our switchboard cut off all the other callers who were waiting. Is there anything else you would like to ask Mr Mandela? But just before you do, Sam, I just want to tell the listeners to call now with their questions for Nelson Mandela; the lines are open. Okay, Sam, go fit it.'

'Thank you, Tim. Actually, Tata Mandela, my question to you is a simple one. I want to ask you about your children. You know,

Tata, I only have one child, Rephile. Despite your hardships, you have been lucky, Makgatho, Makaziwe, Thembi, Zindziswa, Zenani, so many children. I want to ask you a difficult question…'

'Go ahead, Sam, and please make it quick, I can see our lines flashing again here in the studio.'

'Okay, Tim, I want to ask Tata Mandela: how can a father be a father when he is far away all the time, in prison maybe? Was it not difficult for you to earn the respect of your children?'

It was still dark when he woke. The darkness, however, was retreating. Some drivers had already switched their engines on. He needed to pee again. His mouth was dry too. Climbing from the truck, he thought about his conversation with Mandela. It had seemed so real, the difficult stammering out of his question, the peculiar manner in which the great man had started answering his question. What had he asked again? The clarity of the dream was quickly retreating, leaving him with only suggestive outlines. He passed a truck that looked like the one Moses had described to him last night. Its curtains were still drawn, the windows steamed over with vapour.

Sam greeted a man stooped over the washbasin as he entered the bathroom area. He looked at himself in the mirror, at the company logo he wore on his chest. I'm old … just like Mandela. He splashed his face, briskly wiping it with a small cloth afterwards. Looking at himself again as he brushed his teeth, he decided he would eat further along the road. There was nothing left for him here.

The vast, open tract of gravel where he had parked his truck was a mess. Discarded mielie cobs, empty nips of brandy, old cellular phone cards, the sun-bleached core of what looked like a mango pip, even cow dung littered the ground. He stepped over a tyre impression pressed into the earth by a truck. It had hardened in the sun, leaving a permanent spoor on the land. He was lucky he hadn't tripped over one of them last night, he thought; they were everywhere.

He saw Neo approaching.

'Good morning.' He tried to sound upbeat.

She walked towards him with a defiant look in her eyes. It was as if the early-morning light had rendered him entirely invisible.

'Good morning,' he repeated. She stopped, almost smiled.

'Hello, Papa Crocs.' Her mouth blossomed with a wistful smile. She resumed walking.

The gears of his truck grated as he shifted into second. It was as if his truck, which lurched momentarily, was also waking up. He passed the truck where Moses lay sleeping. No urgency, just a piecemeal job, he had said. Who could blame him? Sam accelerated, swivelling the steering wheel manically to make the wide, arcing turn. He thought he saw Neo smoking on the stoep by the Yebo Yes sign. As he steered the truck out of the yard, he looked into his mirror. All he saw was the outline of someone, vague and fleeting.

He fidgeted with his radio. What was it he had read in Mandela's book, that thing about the challenge that confronts every prisoner? He couldn't remember. In any case, it was too early for such thoughts. Looking at his clock, Sam calculated that he would reach Newcastle early this afternoon: home, though, was still impossibly far off.

Incident report

'Not the books.'

'But it will look stupid, Liezel.'

'It doesn't matter, I don't want to move the books.'

'But I hardly think someone who lives in a shack would have a collection of computer programming books on their shelf.'

'It doesn't matter, Ronel.'

'Ag, come on, Liezel. It's going to spoil the first impression when people arrive at the party. We can move the bookcase to your room, just for tonight.'

'I'm not going to argue about this, okay. The books stay!'

'Suit yourself, then, but just so that you know, I think it looks stupid.'

Liezel and Ronel van Vuuren stepped back and looked at the lounge. But for the bookshelf, all the contents of the lounge had been removed to the stoep. It had taken most of the morning, but they were nearly done. The walls were now completely covered over with newspapers and promotional pullouts. Even the curtains had been changed, the mismatched drapes blackened in the oven, for effect.

'What do you think?'

'I still think the bookcase should go.'

'I said no.'

'It's not like you're going to offend Jaco or anything. It's been five years now.'

'Just leave it.'

Liezel walked off. She sat down on a barstool in the open-plan kitchen. The appearance was close enough, she thought, looking at the book lying open on the counter top.

'Go call Mig.'

'He's still sleeping,' answered Ronel.

'Well, I think it's time he chips in a bit. I can't move those big couches back inside, I still have to go to Pick 'n Pay.'

'When are you going?'

'Now.'

'Can you get me some Grandpas when you go?' Ronel asked, sitting down opposite her older sister. She looked at the upside-down photograph in the book, an interior of a shack dwelling, a kitchen.

'Where were you last night?' Liezel asked. She closed the book. *Shack Style*.

'News Café.'

'With Mig?'

'Ja.'

She shifted the book to one side.

'Look, I know it's none of my business but just don't let Andries find out, not tonight at least.'

'He won't.'

As her sister's car reversed out of the garage, Ronel knocked on the bedroom door.

'Wake up, sleepy,' she said, sticking her head through the door.

Miguel Fernandez rubbed his eyes, sat upright in the small bed. It was a single bed in a children's room. A large Disney puzzle (500 pieces) was suspended above it.

'Shit, what time is it?'

'Almost lunch time.' She sat down on the edge of the bed.

'What time did you get here?'

'Oh, early. I had to help Liezel with the decorations for the party. It will totally freak you out when you see what we've done.'

'Why?'

'It totally looks like the inside of a shack.' Her hand playfully touched his foot, which poked out from under the duvet.

'Come lie next to me,' he said, moving up against the wall. He was shirtless.

'I can't.'

He tickled at her side with his big toe. She crawled in next to him. His embrace was warm.

'I have to go.'

'Why?'

'I have to pick Andries up at the airport.'

'I thought he was coming back next week.'

'Change of plan. Apparently they're ahead of schedule, for some or other reason. They can't do anything on site until one of the subcontractors finishes, so he decided to come back.'

Miguel touched the nape of her neck, ran his fingers through her loose length of hair.

'Don't, I can't stay. I'm already late.' Ronel stood up. Miguel hastily shifted his posture in the bed to hide his erection. Ignoring it, she looked at the illustrated characters in the framed scene. She could name almost all of them. Somehow, this annoyed her.

'Do you want something to drink?'

'Coffee, please.'

'I'll put the kettle on for you as I leave.'

By the time he had finished showering Ronel had already left. The water in the kettle was only lukewarm. He switched the kettle on again. Liezel had left him a note on top of a hardcover book. It asked if he could move the couches back into the lounge. As he waited for the kettle to boil, he flicked through the book. He paused on a photograph of a woman standing in her garden.

Her name was Patience Manyisa, 38. *I love my garden. I like to grow spinach and other vegetables. My favourite flower is a geranium.* That's all it said. The kettle came to a boil. He closed the book, turned it over to look for the price. What did people pay for crap like this?

Coffee in hand, Miguel strolled into the lounge. Maids and garden boys, Liezel had told him at dinner a few weeks back. No one had ever come up with that idea for a fancy-dress party before. He had simply laughed, thought she was joking.

Why hadn't they shifted the bookshelf? It looked stupid with all those books stuck slap bang in the middle of the lounge. Maybe they had left it for him to move, although she hadn't written anything in the note? Nor had Ronel said anything. He walked and stood in front of the tall, pine bookcase.

The books were alphabetically ordered: BETA, C++, COBOL, Delphi, Fortran, Java, Linux, Objective-C, Pascal, Unix. It was just like Jaco to order things this way.

Looking at the newsprint covering the lounge wall, he calculated how long it had been since Jaco died in the car accident on the highway. Miguel was still in Dubai, then, hadn't been able to get off work for the funeral. Was it 1998? He couldn't remember. Ignoring the column of black smoke rising above the city of Baghdad, he briefly concentrated on the photograph of a young Menlo Park Hoër pupil. She was headed for Europe with her mountain bike. Pretty. Pick 'n Pay had recently had a special on tuna. Patrice Motsepe was at loggerheads with the management of Sundowns. So many names he couldn't even pronounce these days. A photograph of a balaclava-clad man dressed in prison orange made him stop.

WHO IS MZEKEZEKE? He stumbled on the pronunciation of the name, swallowed a mouthful of coffee, then read the small caption accompanying the photograph. *Some say he comes from Mnonjaneng section in Thembisa, on the East Rand, but insiders from the music industry are now saying that the masked pop star is actually Yfm's DJ S'bu Leopeng and a resident of Dainfern.* Dainfern? Wasn't that that expensive place in Jo'burg, near Fourways? He wasn't sure. Even after two months back in the country he still felt totally out of touch. It didn't help that Liezel lived in a cluster village on the far edge of Pretoria.

The bookshelf was heavy. He tried pushing it but it wouldn't budge. He would have to unpack the shelf and move everything separately. The books were surprisingly heavy and plentiful. It took a number of trips up and down the passage before he had transferred all of them into the study, where he piled them on the floor, next to some unopened boxes and a basket filled with ironing. The bookshelf went onto the stoep. Returning to the bare lounge, he looked at the rectangular section of wall. They had plastered the newsprint around the shelving.

The newspapers were stored under the kitchen sink, and he set about covering the exposed section of wall. He was almost done when he paused on a half-completed crossword puzzle. It was Liezel's handwriting. Eight down was still incomplete. He looked at the clue. Obscure (9 letters). What kind of clue was that? The word obviously started with the letter *r* though, six across having the word 'construct' neatly penned into the blocks. What is another word for obscure? He had no idea, stood up; Liezel had just pulled up in her car.

'Jesus, it's only been two hours and already you're acting like a kaffir,' said Andries. Ronel had just dropped a glass. Everyone laughed.

Andries was dressed in a blue overall. Having never met him before, Miguel couldn't be sure how different he looked from normal – his face was completely covered in black. Miguel scratched his leg. It itched in the cheap pair of trousers he had borrowed. He also wore a white button shirt, black waistcoat and Savoy Dobbs hat: the gardener-going-home look, he had told Liezel just before the first guests arrived. She had spent much of the afternoon crying.

Ronel returned with a broom and dustpan.

'Look at her. She knows how to play the part, doesn't she?' It was Andries.

'Shut up!'

'And cheeky too, just like all of them nowadays.'

The partygoers, who numbered about twenty, all adults if you excluded Liezel's daughter and three other children, laughed. As she sullenly swept the floor, the disparate conversations resumed. Not knowing many of the visitors, Miguel found himself silently listening, a spectator of the festivities rather than a participant. He excused himself.

Sitting on the toilet he leafed through a magazine, *Cosmopolitan*. He had tried most of the naughty office positions, as the sex feature described them. Not with South African women, though, although he had done the Boardroom Twist with Ronel on Liezel's dining-room table a few afternoons back. She bored him. Everything about her bored him: her drunken monologues, the uninspired groping and moaning during sex. Liezel was a much better option, although after the way she had screamed at him when she got home, he would have to play it easy with her if he wanted to keep his room. He needed something that was rent-free while he sorted his life out. He flushed the toilet.

The get-up was absurd, he thought, looking at the black face paint, dabbing at a thickened patch on his cheekbone. He tilted his hat off centre, opened the door.

'I was wondering where you'd disappeared to.' It was Ronel. She giggled as she pushed Miguel back, shutting the door quickly then locking it.

'It's almost like you've been avoiding me.' She was drunk again.

'Don't be stupid, your husband's here.'

'You heard how he treats me.'

'What if he catches you?'

'You mean us.' She tapped at the tip of his nose.

When she arrived at the party earlier, with Andries, he had not recognised her at first. Only after Liezel's daughter cried out 'Auntie Ronel' did he realise it was her. She had gone to a lot of effort for the party, wrapping a headscarf over an Afro. The wig looked silly but it had tricked him, even made him laugh afterwards.

'I didn't realise he was *such* an arsehole,' Miguel whispered. She moved closer. There was nowhere left to retreat.

'I don't feel like talking about him. Just hold me.'

He ran his hand across the contours of her back as she nestled in his embrace. The pink dress she wore, a domestic's outfit, was made from a cheap acrylic fabric. He thought of the woman with her flowers he had seen in the book earlier, tried to dismiss it by concentrating on the unspoken gestures of her body as she pushed it up against him. He kissed her. Her mouth tasted of red wine.

She wasn't wearing any panties underneath her outfit. He entered her silently, Ronel sitting on top.

'Oh Christ, look at my face,' she blurted when she looked at herself in the mirror afterwards. Parts of her neck and face were showing her true skin colour: white. Miguel had bitten at her neck as he climaxed.

'I look a mess.'

So did he. Looking at his reflection, he saw that his face had exposed bits of white showing where the sweat had run from his forehead. He watched Ronel massage away the blotches with a circular motion of her hand, making herself black again. He motioned to kiss her shoulder but abruptly resisted. He splashed his face with water.

'What are you doing?'

'I feel stupid like this,' he replied. The face paint did not come off very easily.

'No more stupid than any of us.'

A high-pitched sound suddenly filled the air. It was the alarm. They heard giggles outside the door, followed by hasty footsteps.

'It must be those fucking kids.'

'Do you think they heard us?' she asked, her voice panicky.

'I dunno, but you better slip out quickly.' He bundled her out of the door.

The alarm drew some of the party guests into the house, and he heard Andries shouting over the noise of the alarm. And then, as swiftly as it had started, the sound of the alarm disappeared.

He heard footsteps coming down the passage.

'It wasn't me, *baas*,' Miguel said, responding to the knock on the door. Someone laughed. Andries? He waited a while longer. He heard the telephone ring. It was the security company.

It took two more attempts before he got most of the stuff off his face. Walking down the passage, he licked his thumb and rubbed at the small blemishes he had seen still marking his face as he exited the bathroom.

'Look at this one, he got such a fright that he turned white.' It was Andries.

Soon, the excitement tapered off and everyone returned outside. The newspapers had been a waste, Miguel thought as he followed the group. Someone took his seat. He sat on a concrete ledge, listening as one of the guests complained how his neighbour's alarm always went off in the dead of night, waking up the whole neighbourhood. Jaco's sister then asked how much Liezel was paying for her security. The question sparked a vibrant exchange. Things were back to normal. The delicate shell of their lie was still intact.

'Mig, can you get it?' Liezel ordered when the doorbell rang. She was still brusque with him.

The short, rather portly man was dressed in a khaki uniform, a small badge pinned to his chest. S. Motswane introduced himself by the name of his company, Bateleur Security.

'It was just a false alarm. We're having a bit of a party and the kids were mucking about.'

'I have to inspect the house.' He was polite but firm.

'Sure, come in.' Mig showed S. Motswane into the lounge. He realised there was little use in trying to explain the décor, or the food heaped in mismatching plastic containers. Not even the small ANC flag suspended from the ceiling light.

'I must also check outside,' he stated after returning from cursorily inspecting the bedrooms. Miguel led him to the stoep.

'You're a bit late for the party, *boeta*.' It was Andries, again. S. Motswane edged his way past the guests into the garden. His torch momentarily paused on a section of the wall where the razor wire was weighed down by a granadilla creeper before he disappeared around the corner, a crackle of static from his walkie-talkie the only indication that S. Motswane hadn't slipped over a wall and simply left. Someone, the man seated next to Andries mentioned spotting a Bateleur eagle on his last trip to the Kruger Park; S. Motswane reappeared around the corner. He switched off his torch as he approached the seated group. Ronel – almost guiltily, Miguel thought – thanked him for coming. This sparked a chorus of drunken thanks and greetings, Andries grabbing his hand. S. Motswane flinched.

'I'm sorry if we wasted your time,' Miguel offered as he ushered him through the front door. The man simply nodded his head, returned to his bakkie.

The patrol vehicle was double-parked behind some of the visitors' cars. Miguel waited to wave him off; it seemed the least he could do for wasting his time. S. Motswane was in no hurry to leave. After speaking into his two-way radio he switched on his cabin light, leaning over and reaching for something on the floor. Miguel walked across to where the bakkie was parked.

'What's that you're filling out?'

'An incident report.'

'Do you have to fill it out even if nothing happens?'

S. Motswane looked up from the yellow gloom of the interior. 'Yes.'

'And what will you say?'

He ignored the question, instead concentrating on awkwardly balancing the logbook on the bakkie's steering wheel.

He started completing the report in a neat blue script; first the date, then the time, followed by Liezel's residential address: Unit 18, Maldoror Mews. He paused on the last column, a substantial blank space where the incident was described.

'What will you write?' Miguel asked, squinting to read the list of previous comments. They were a systematic record of predictability, each written in the same hand – in upper-case letters. The glide of S. Motswane's pen repeated the terse mantra: 'FALSE ALARM – NO PROBLEM.'

Walking back to the house, Miguel wondered whether anyone at Bateleur Security – a supervisor maybe – ever scrutinised these documents, or if they merely existed for insurance investigators and sales representatives from document storage companies. He thought about S. Motswane. What would his unofficial report be of the night's events at Unit 18, Maldoror Mews? What would he tell his colleagues, the uniformed men who huddled in parked vehicles at intersections exchanging cigarettes late at night, waiting? That he had visited a suburban party where things had been wistfully strange?

Locking the front door on these thoughts, Miguel spotted the face paint still accumulated on the underside of his fingernails. It was black and incriminating. He ducked into the kitchen. Steam from the faucet eventually blurred his reflection in the window as he stood waiting for the water to heat up. He thrust his hands beneath its steady flow. The scalding heat, however, offered no penance, nor did the intensity with which he scrubbed at his fingers.

His cuticles bleeding, Miguel returned to the party outside. The conversation had moved along from the false alarm,

Liezel smiling benignly at him as he sat down. All the wood was spent and the fire was now slowly dwindling into a red glow of coals. Andries placed his hand on Ronel's knee.

The trophy mount

'Marie tried to kill herself,' said Danny, sitting himself upright in the small A-frame tent. I slipped into the tent next to him. He had a thick layer of white cream covering his sunburnt nose and his red curls were greasy and unkempt. He wasn't designed for the sun or December holidays camping by the beach. Closing the comic book he had been reading, he laconically continued with his explanation of the vomit trail that led from the two-lane dirt track to the Walker campsite.

'She drank all Uncle Kenny's booze.'

'Why'd she do that?' I asked.

'I dunno, she's crazy.'

I chuckled, describing in detail the large black ants I had seen probing at the edges of the sticky mess. I told him how I had poked at it with a long piece of grass.

'Sick, man!' he laughed, turning over onto his stomach again and opening his comic book. I tucked in next to him.

I first met Danny three years ago, a few months after my dad's panel beating shop signed a deal with the company his father worked for. Since then, every December, we would meet at Sodwana Bay, on the northern KwaZulu-Natal coast. It was a strange paradise, the campsites wedged between a crocodile-infested mangrove swamp and conservation land that had once been used as a missile testing range. The two of us struck up an uncomplicated friendship, largely because we were the same age, and from Pretoria, although he lived in the north, near Sinoville. I went to school in Lyttleton, in the south. The only other time we ever saw each other during the year was at the annual inter-schools athletic meet, but we hardly spoke then, keeping to our school friends.

My younger brother thought he was a nerd and sometimes teased him about his freckles. I was not as outgoing as my younger brother, who always made friends amongst the children playing in the brackish lagoon near the beach. Danny was also easy enough to get along with. Often we would spend time under his mother's sun umbrella talking, his older sister, Belinda, pitching in with some or other sulky comment. Sometimes, though, we would walk along the beach, usually in the late afternoon, studying the tracks. Danny was a pro and could identify most of the competing tyre manufacturers by their distinctive treads: Yokohama Super Diggers, Goodyear Wranglers, BF Goodrich All Terrains, even the really expensive Pirelli Scorpion Zeroes. I was always amazed.

'My dad said I can't go fishing with him tomorrow,' Danny mumbled. He was pulling at a loose piece of skin on his nose while reading his comic.

'Why?'

'Because of Uncle Kenny.'

'But I thought your dad said you could go fishing with him this year.'

'Well, that's what he said in Pretoria, but now he says he's worried that I'll get sick if I'm in the sun the whole day.'

'Maybe he's right.'

'No, he just wants me off the boat so that Uncle Kenny's friend can go fishing.'

'Too bad.'

'I hate him.' I wasn't sure who he meant and continued reading.

I first met Uncle Kenny, or Kenny Andrews, at a big braai when we first came to Sodwana. Uncle Kenny was nearly 40, although he looked much older. Unlike Marie, his young girlfriend, he had dark, malevolent eyes, their colour not dissimilar to the brackish water that trickled from the swamp into the sea. He owned a fleet of tow trucks, which Danny's father managed. KT Services. The name was painted all over both his and Danny's dad's bakkies.

'Kenny's Towing Services?' I had asked Danny at the braai.

'No, King Thick,' he had whispered with an evil smile. It was round about then that I decided I would befriend him. It didn't matter that he was a bit geeky.

'Why did Marie try to kill herself?' I asked, turning the page of the comic I was reading, *Tintin in Tibet*.

'She was depressed, or something.'

'Why was she depressed?'

'I don't know. I heard my mom say it's because she is so much younger than him. They can't relate, or something like that.'

'Sounds weird.'

'Ja, they're messed up.'

I laughed at Danny's quip and returned to the comic book. A wafer of skin landed on Snowy. It was the piece Danny had been pulling at the whole time.

'Grim!' I screeched. Danny simply laughed. I sat up and flicked it out of the tent. 'You're sick, you know that.'

We continued reading in silence.

'Belinda saw it happen,' Danny remarked, sitting upright.

'Saw what?'

'Uncle Kenny beating up Marie.'

'Really,' I said, intrigued. 'What happened?'

'She won't tell me but I heard her telling her friends about it. I think he tied her up to a tree and punched her a few times.'

'*That's* messed up,' I declared.

'What is?'

'Uncle Kenny and Marie.'

'I suppose. In any case, he's a dick.'

Closing the book on Captain Haddock, I looked at Danny. He was sitting, quietly staring through the entrance at the wild bushes and undergrowth outside the tent.

'What are you looking at?'

'Nothing,' he replied, his sunburn luminescent in the late afternoon light.

'I bet Uncle Kenny's sailfish is bigger than that shark.' Danny pointed to the large mako shark strung from the wooden trusses used to weigh game fish landed at the bay. The angler, a squat man with a perfectly round belly, beamed at the crowd gathered around his catch.

'No ways,' I countered. It was obvious that the shark was bigger.

'Yes ways.' Danny pushed me a little too intently. In turn, I flicked his floppy white hat off his head.

'Not funny!' Reaching for his hat, he quickly covered his sweaty, red curls.

'You look like you've got radiation sickness,' my young brother laughed, running off to the lagoon.

'Ha, ha, very funny,' he shouted after him, pulling his hat low over his face, which was smothered with sun block.

'Don't mind him, he's always a pain.'

Danny sullenly made his way to the front of the assembled crowd to get a closer view of the shark being lowered onto an open-top bakkie. I scanned the crowd. I had not seen Belinda since the night I had left Danny's tent. She wasn't here, it seemed. I pushed forward.

'Look.'

It was Uncle Kenny's silver-blue sailfish. They were hoisting it by its tail, its long, spear-like snout pointed to the ground. It was definitely longer than the shark but also much thinner.

'Marie, did you remember to bring the camera from the campsite?' It was Uncle Kenny.

Wearing a flowing caftan and dark glasses, Marie said nothing.

'Marie! Did you remember the camera?'

Her face was expressionless, although even from where I was I could see the hint of discolouration peeking beneath the left lens of her glasses, a bruise.

'No,' she finally answered, turning and walking off towards the beach.

'What's up with her?' I asked Danny.

'I dunno.'

I looked up at the suspended fish. A slow trickle of blood dripped from its mouth. It formed a crimson stain on the beach sand beneath it.

Uncle Kenny had to ask my dad to take a photo of his fish. He had been so mad after that, and raced off alone with his catch to the cleaning area. Danny and I had to walk up. When we arrived at the makeshift cleaning spot, a concrete foundation with some taps and a basin, Uncle Kenny was speaking to a man dressed in a khaki safari outfit, a family man, not a fisherman.

'It looks like a female,' he authoritatively told the man.

'Can you eat it?' He had a foreign accent.

'No, jusus, this meat's *kak*. I'm just going to cut off its head. The Parks Board kaffirs will eat the meat. They mos eat anything.' The man looked at Uncle Kenny in an uncertain way, then retreated.

The dead fish still had the green, glitter-streaked lure that had enticed it hooked through the corner of its beak.

'She was a tough bitch,' Uncle Kenny stated, looking at me. He had never spoken directly to me before. I smiled nervously.

'Look here.' He held out his hand to me, showing me his palm. It had a huge blood blister. I looked at his other hand. He wore two gold rings on that one.

Bending over, he rummaged through his tackle box, removing a rusty knife with a long blade. After scraping it against the cement (a horrible sound), he offered it to me.

'Here, I'll give you the honours. You can cut her belly open.'

'No, that's okay.' I recoiled.

'Suit yourself.' He stuck the knife in the fish's soft underbelly and hacked it open. The contents spilt out over the wet concrete surface. Seagulls dipped and dived and squawked overhead. The sky was full of them.

I wandered off to look at the other, smaller fish caught that day. I stopped in front of the spindle-shaped body of a tuna. It had a dark metallic blue sheen and lay stiffly on the cement. Neatly laid out next to it were two pickhandle barracuda, both roughly the same size. I hunched down to view the pair. Their large black eyes were intently focused on the sky above.

'Bet you won't touch its eye.' It was Belinda's voice. I knew it even before I looked up.

'Oh yes I will.' I gingerly ran my finger across the slippery meniscus of the fish's eye.

'Sis! What does it feel like?'

'It's nothing. Try it.'

She knelt down next to me. I felt a sudden tremor of excitement. Belinda was two years older than me. She always had a charming smell about her, of coconut oil and danger. She was a vicious gossip. Whenever we went to braai at the Walker's campsite, Belinda would tell fanciful stories to all the children. Her stories intrigued me, largely because she was the singular highlight of my holidays in Sodwana.

She tentatively directed her finger at the fish.

'Hey, get away from those fish,' an angry fisherman shouted from his 4x4. We retreated, giggling.

'They're so damn precious about their fish,' Belinda said as she gingerly made her way through a mess of entrails, fish gills and flies. We were headed towards Uncle Kenny. He was trying, with some difficulty it seemed, to cut off the fish's head. We stopped and silently watched.

'I saw what he did to Marie,' Belinda whispered in my ear. Her breath smelt of Coke – it was heavenly. I glanced up at her, at the lone freckle on the tip of her nose. She smiled.

'I was there.'

'You mean you saw him punch her?'

'Amongst other things.'

'Like what?'

'Wouldn't you like to know.'

'Ag, come on. Don't be like that.'

She walked off in the direction of the basin and peered into it. She wrinkled her nose.

'Oh come on, tell me.'

'Only if you say please.' She was enjoying my begging.

'Please!'

'And only if you put your hand inside this mush.' She pointed to the leftovers of a fish with her slender, big toe. The blood-streaked muck was covered in flies.

'Okay,' I said and promptly stuck my finger into it. It was cold.

'Gross,' she squealed. 'That was obviously too easy.'

'No ways, I did what you asked and now you must tell.'

'And what if I don't.'

'Then I'll chuck this on you.' I motioned to pick up the mess of guts I had just stuck my finger into.

'No sick, don't,' she giggled.

'Well then, tell me what you saw.'

'Okay, okay.'

She walked in the direction of the headless sailfish. He had finished. Uncle Kenny had got his trophy.

'Okay, I'll tell you but only if you, hmmm … put the fish's heart in your mouth.'

'No stuff that. This isn't *Fear Factor*, you know.'

'So we're quits then?' she declared sulkily. 'I don't have to tell you anything.'

I kneeled down in front of the wasted fish.

'I don't even know what a fish's heart looks like.'

'So you'll do it?' She was sceptical.

'Yes.'

'Cool! We studied anatomy this year. We even did a dissection of a rat.'

It took quite a while before we found a discarded ice-cream stick – and Danny. The three of us returned to the fish. With her sun-bleached length of hair tied up behind her head, Belinda tentatively sifted through the guts of the fish with the ice-cream stick.

'Here it is!' She pointed to a purple bit of meat. It looked bigger than I had expected. A bitter taste formed in my mouth.

'Yuck, I can't put all of that in my mouth.'

'Chicken,' Danny lashed out viciously.

'Stuff you!' I poked my finger at the fish's organ, tried to lift the heart out of the sodden mess. It was impossible;

the whole of the spilt mess seemed to move with it.

'I'll get a knife,' Danny said, running off.

'You better tell me what you saw after I do this,' I demanded sternly, looking at Belinda. My eyes momentarily dropped down.

'Stop staring!'

'I wasn't,' I stated defensively, blushing. I had been caught out. She glowered at me, then tucked her left hand into her right armpit, in effect shielding her small breasts from view. I knew I had just ruined all of my efforts in a momentary waver of my eye; I would have to put the fish's heart in my mouth.

Danny returned with the rusty knife Uncle Kenny had used to open the fish. It was very blunt but I eventually managed to hack a small parcel of flesh from the heart, if it was what it was. I held it out in the palm of my hand. Belinda and Danny curiously touched it, almost as if it were still living. It definitely felt dead.

'Okay, so repeat the deal.' I had never really noticed how much taller Belinda was than me.

'If you put that in your mouth, I'll tell you what I saw Uncle Kenny do to Marie.'

'And maybe she'll even give you a kiss,' Danny added sarcastically. 'We all know that's all you really want.'

'Ag!'

'Is it a deal?' Belinda asked.

'Deal,' I said, offering her my left hand. We shook on it. It was the first time I had ever touched her in such a determined way. It was exciting.

'Now do it.'

I stuck my tongue out, delicately placing the piece of flesh onto my tongue.

'I said inside your mouth,' Belinda ordered. 'You have to close your mouth on it.'

I shook my head vigorously but knew the hopelessness of trying to negotiate now as she stood there staring at me wide-eyed. I closed my eyes and slowly, carefully drew my tongue in. I shouldn't have closed my eyes.

Belinda jumped forward. With a carefully aimed blow she slammed my jaw shut. I bit into the thing in my mouth. It tasted bloody.

'You fucked-up bitch,' I yelled after spitting the mass of flesh out. I had never used the f-word so coldly before.

No matter how much I spat, retched or gargled at a tap, I could not get rid of the dark taste in my mouth. The sight of fly-encrusted innards nearby also made me vomit. A short distance behind me, I heard Belinda laughing, Danny too. I could feel the tears welling, and quickly stuck my head under the tap. I soaked my whole upper body.

'What are you doing?' It was Danny.

'Nothing, just mess off.'

'It was only a joke.' Belinda had also come closer.

'You're messed up! Both of you.'

'You said you wanted to know what happened so I thought I'd show you.' Belinda laughed cruelly.

'You're sick!'

'Not as sick as Uncle Kenny. He used his boat rope to tie her to the tree before he hit her. He kept calling her a drunk and a whore.'

The story didn't seem to matter any more. It had never been about the stupid, sick story, anyway. I wiped at a tear running down my cheek.

'She did that too,' remarked Belinda snidely.

It just happened automatically, a reflex action. I dug my hand into a pile of fish innards and flung them at her. It splattered all over her belly and legs, even staining parts of her yellow bikini bottom.

'You pig!' She burst into tears and ran off.

'My dad's gonna get you,' Danny said vengefully.

'Get lost, radiation freak!' I watched as he ran along the dirt track leading to his campsite.

For a while I loitered around the cleaning area, watching as the gulls fought over bits of fish. Sometimes they even fought in the sky, making elaborate pirouettes as they squabbled over leftover bits of fish. Eventually, two men in Parks Board overalls and gumboots arrived on a tractor. They hosed down the cleaning area, finally left with Uncle Kenny's fish loaded onto their trailer.

It was the night before we were due to go back to Pretoria. New Year's Eve. A big braai. Red meat and loud talk. My mom and dad were there, also my younger brother. The Walkers too – all of them. And Uncle Kenny, with Marie, although the two weren't talking, not to each other at least. There were others as well, mostly Uncle Kenny's friends, rough men who soldiered through the beer with stories of big fish and unpredictable seas. It almost sounded heroic as I listened in on the talk.

Just before the kids' dinner, cutlets and boerewors, I was hauled in front of an impromptu jury: Mrs Walker, my mom and Marie. What had happened the other day? Why weren't we speaking to one another? I told my version, Belinda and Danny theirs. None of us mentioned Uncle Kenny or Marie. 'Is!' 'Isn't.' We argued ourselves into a corner, unable to get past the impasse; we were lying just to avoid shaming Marie. Finally, Danny broke down. A slender version of the truth came out, something about the vomit near the tent. Marie winced. The women were all embarrassed.

'You should mind your own business, young man,' my mother said, pinching my side hard. It hurt, but I gulped down the pain. I would have a bruise the next day.

As I sulkily walked with my dinner plate looking for somewhere to sit near the fire, I saw Belinda crying over her food. I knew she was crying; her shoulders were trembling. Her mother had slapped her in the face, right in front of all of us. I didn't know what to say and walked past. I sat near Danny.

'I'm sorry for calling you that name.'

'It's okay,' he replied, picking at his food.

We ate in silence. After dinner he showed me a new comic book he had got from his grandmother for Christmas. The big day had come glumly a day after the flare-up at the fish cleaning area. We didn't talk about it.

It was my younger brother who came and whispered into our ears, telling us to come look. He even invited Belinda. Marie had passed out in a fold-up chair in front of the fire, her head leaning heavily to one side. On the ground next to her lay an empty glass. We sat in a huddle nearby, pretending to be looking at something in the ground. The light of the fire glowed through the underside of her chair, which was exactly why my brother had chosen this spot. He pointed at the base of the chair.

'What is it?' Belinda asked.

'Pee,' my brother whispered. It dripped slowly from underneath the chair. There was something sad about it, I thought, trying not to think of the blood dripping out of the sailfish's mouth.

'Ah, no man, sis!' Danny hissed.

We each took turns looking at Marie's humiliation. Mostly we said nothing; we had all learnt not to involve adults in our world. We all giggled when my brother threw a round seed pod at Marie. It hit her on the head, but she remained motionless.

'Do you know what?' Belinda said hesitantly. I looked raptly at her, the broken firelight dancing on her face.

'What?' I asked when no one else did.

'Remember that fish Uncle Kenny caught? The sailfish.' We all nodded our heads. 'Apparently he had to chuck the head away, this morning.'

'Why?' my brother asked.

'It had rotted in his deepfreeze.'

'But how's that possible?' I asked.

Belinda smiled, a mixture of unrestrained malice and quiet understanding, then told us her latest secret.

'I heard my dad telling my mom that Marie switched his deep freeze off, to spite him or something. My dad says Uncle Kenny only found out about it today, when he went to the place where they keep all the freezers. Everything was *vrot* by then.'

'What did he do with the head?' I asked.

'I don't know. Why don't you go ask him?'

Things were returning to normal. Shortly afterwards, my brother and Danny started arguing. I asked Belinda if she wanted to go look for the fish's head. No, she said, brushing past me in a scented huff. Midnight came soon afterwards, a joyous noise of firecrackers, car hooters and laughter. Marie slept through it all.